BEVERLEY GREEN: SASQUATCH HUNTER

BOOK ONE OF THE BEVERLEY GREEN CHRONICLES

ANDREA C. NEIL

For the muses

ONE

I wiped the sweat from my temple with my shirtsleeve and looked down at my jeans. There were splotches of chicken poop all over them, and I wasn't even half-done yet. This was proving to be one hell of a messy morning. I asked myself the question, the one that went something like, why on earth did I move here?

I'd asked myself this question a billion times since I moved back to Oklahoma four months earlier. And I'd asked myself this question about a thousand times just in the last hour. Looking down at my jeans again, I knew they would be completely covered with poop by the time I was done. I sighed heavily, like I was contemplating world peace or what to eat for dinner. But no, I was just chasing chickens. Literally chasing chickens. Down the street. This was not quite the picture of suburban domestic bliss I had envisioned when I'd decided to move. I admit, I had decided I would own chickens before I even put my Manhattan apartment up for sale, but in hindsight I'd had an overly romantic idea of what it would be like. I imagined happy, quiet animals that would

1

provide me with breakfast fixins. But reality had panned out a little differently, and I had ended up with a gang of surly, suspicious hens that spent the majority of their time plotting escape and revenge. There were definitely no poop-covered jeans anywhere in that vision I had of my new life. But real life was messy, and I should have known better.

My name is Beverley Green, and I live in Guthrie, Oklahoma. I moved back here to Oklahoma from New York City. I had first moved there to go to college, but after I graduated with a master's in English from NYU, I ended up staying. I worked my way into a great publishing job and had been making a decent living as an editor. I had a decent apartment in a decent Manhattan neighborhood, too. And then earlier this year, I gave it all up to chase chickens around a suburban Oklahoma neighborhood.

The chickens had gotten out of their coop sometime in the early-morning hours, because they were all fine when I'd checked on them before bed last night. This was the second time they'd escaped in as many weeks. I blamed it all on Beryl—a feisty Catalana who was the ringleader of the chicken gang that called my backyard home. Her peers had officially voted her "hen most likely to incite a riot." I swear she knew how to pick (or is that peck?) open the latch on the pen. It was as if she'd heard the call of the open road beckoning like a hot rooster shaking his tail feathers her direction. Needing to feel the late-summer Oklahoma breeze on her wattle, she'd probably made her move as soon as the sun had come up on this beautiful Monday morning.

Beryl had opened the pen and somehow managed to hop the chain-link fence that separated the yard from the driveway. As I was washing my breakfast dishes, I looked out the window over the sink and saw several birds wandering aimlessly in the yard; perhaps they had stayed behind because they were too chicken to follow their leader. The rest of the birds, eight to be exact, were nowhere to be seen.

Oh great, I thought. Now I was going to be late for work. I ran outside as fast as I could and grabbed the closest birds, throwing them back in the pen and closing the gate behind them. They were easy to catch—they probably knew they'd be no match for me so hadn't bothered trying to make a break for it. I reckoned that they had just wished the others luck and asked for souvenirs.

I walked out of the backyard and looked around, spotting three more of my chickens right in the front yard. Maybe this wouldn't be so bad after all. I stopped to create a quick plan, knowing I didn't have much time to spare. Should I go for these chickens, or should I look for the ones that were farthest away? If I wasn't careful, I could lose some of my hens to dogs, cats, or hungry neighbors who might have been under the false impression that I was giving away free chicken dinners. And I knew Beryl would be the farthest away. Maybe it would be best if I just let her have her freedom. But no, I wanted everyone home safe, even the trouble-maker. It shouldn't be this hard, I found myself thinking. Again.

I made a snap decision, and in the interest of saving time, I headed straight toward the birds that were in the front yard, thinking I could just scoop them up before they realized what was happening. But again, I should have known better. Those chickens were clairvoyant and could feel me coming, so of course they scattered in three different directions, wings flapping everywhere. I thought about the expression "like herding cats." Cats didn't have anything on chickens. I did manage to get two of them before giving up and resorting to my emergency bribing method. Operation Pied Piper commenced.

It took two pounds of organic grapes and some very fancy kitchen scraps to get the rest of the birds home. As predicted, Beryl was the hardest to convince. By the time I found her, she had made it almost all the way to Division Street, the main drag leading to downtown. There was no way I could catch her, so it was a matter of reasoning with her until she realized that no one was going to give her better snacks than me and it would be in her best interest to come on home, where I promised an extra serving of oatmeal would be waiting for her. Not one to go back on my word, once everyone was back home and I had changed out of my poop-laden pants, I whipped up some oatmeal for my chickens. They really had me wrapped around their little fingers. I mean claws.

I passed out snacks to my jailbirds and triple-checked the latch on the pen, satisfied that everyone was safe for the remainder of the day. I made a mental note to search for "chicken-proof gate latches" on the internet that night, convinced (or hopeful, at least) that I couldn't be the only person whose chickens outsmarted them on a regular basis. I stood and watched them milling around. Beryl paced along the fence, staring at me. If she'd had a tin cup, she would have been rattling it along the side of the cage trying to incite her peers to violence. Instead she walked back and forth, eying me suspiciously, laughing her silent chicken laugh.

Yes, today I had asked myself that "why did I move here" question many, many times.

I looked at the time—nine thirty. I'd had breakfast and thwarted the chicken jailbreak, but now I desperately needed a shower. I was going to be late. But instead of stressing about it, I shrugged and decided to make the best of it. When you're the boss, you can cut yourself some slack. I left my poop-covered jeans to ferment on the back porch and headed for the shower.

Even though I was running late, I still decided to walk into town. It was only a mile or so, and the weather was almost perfect. It was late September, one of those days that was still warm, but the sunlight was a little weaker, and the air was a little less humid. Before leaving, I took a look out the open kitchen window and checked on the coop. The chickens were quiet, just milling around slowly, clucking softly, looking for any leftover oatmeal. The breeze picked up and rustled the leaves of the huge oak tree in the corner of the yard. It looked like everything would be all right for the day and that it was safe for me to leave.

As I started gathering up my things, my phone rang. Oh cripes. It was Leona Tisdale, my landlady at work.

"Beverley Green," I answered formally.

"Bev, it's Leona. How are you, sweetie?" Her voice sounded like she was in a good mood. But you never could tell with Leona. It could just as easily be a trap. A sweet, saccharine trap.

"I'm fine, Leona, how are you?" I asked tentatively.

"Oh, I'm all right. The gout in my left big toe is acting up, but I just got these new comfy shoes, so that helps."

I didn't know what to say to this. "Great," was all I could come up with. "So what can I do for you?"

"I just wanted to tell you that someone will be by the shop this afternoon to check the roof. No one else has complained about a roof leak except for you, but I'm having someone stop by to check it, anyway. If you hear someone walking around up there, that's what it is."

5

I knew she didn't believe me that I had a roof leak in the shop, but I did, and if she questioned me again I would save the bucket of smelly water that I'd collected in the back room and leave it on her doorstep. "Okay, that's great, Leona. Thanks for letting me know. It will be nice to have it fixed."

"Okay, sweetie. Oh, and one last thing," she said, her voice becoming just a teeny bit more condescending. "You're still not selling any porn in that shop of yours, right?"

I almost dropped the phone. This was a question she'd asked me several times in the last few months, but it still caught me off guard. "No, ma'am, no porn. Just books."

"And no porny books?" she continued.

"Nope. Everything is as wholesome and salubrious as can be," I assured her. I mean, some romance novels were a bit steamy, but I wasn't sure they technically qualified as porn— at least to someone like me who'd been a book editor in her former life.

"Okay then. You keep things clean in that shop of yours now," and with that she hung up on me.

Okay then! Now I was going to be even later getting the shop open. I grabbed my bag and left the house.

As I walked through my neighborhood toward down-town, I breathed deeply—and started coughing. Fall weather was great, except for the incessant wind that blew all the dust from the summer-parched prairie straight through town. The strong breeze whipped my hair across my face for the hundredth time. I shifted my book bag to the other shoulder and continued walking, trying to admire all the small-town cuteness along the route.

Guthrie is a picturesque little town, just north of the state capital of Oklahoma City, where I was born and raised. Deep down I still thought of myself as an Oklahoma native, even though I'd spent over half my life in New York. I moved back on a whim—or at least what seemed like a whim to everyone else but me. To me, it just seemed like the next logical step, and once I'd made up my mind, why bother putting it off? You can plan stuff all your life. Sometimes you just gotta go and do it.

On the surface, things had been going great in New York. I loved so much about that place—there was so much to do and see and eat and buy. But over the last few years, something began to feel a little off. It was like when you bought a new sweater, and you loved it, and it was your go-to comfy sweater. But the more you wore it, the more you realized that maybe you didn't actually like that particular shade of chartreuse, and the collar kind of felt scratchy on your neck, and the front had started to pill.

Work had always gone well, but one area of my life that hadn't ever gone so great in New York was the relationship thing. To take the sweater analogy further (for better or worse), in the romance department, it was like I never could find a favorite sweater in the first place, and so I never got the chance to get tired of it. I just couldn't find a sweater that fit well enough for it to become my go-to comfy sweater. They were all either too tight or too baggy. No matter how many sweaters I tried on (and I'd tried on a few, just saying), I just couldn't find the perfect one. I was getting kind of tired of looking, to be honest. I'd started to feel like maybe there were better things to do than more sweater shopping in Manhattan.

Then this last spring, I turned forty-five. The morning after my birthday, I woke up alone, with a really spectacular hangover. I had vague memories of a very recent romantic liaison, which was just fancy writer's talk for "last night I had a one-night stand." And as I lay there with my head pounding and my stomach crying uncle, something suddenly changed. I dragged myself out of bed, and in this new light, I assessed my situation. I took a good, long look at all of my sweaters.

There I was, alone in my apartment. A week's worth of laundry—mostly business suits and workout clothes—was piled on the floor at the foot of the bed. A refrigerator, devoid of any nutritional content except for a bottle of expired mustard, stood in the corner of the kitchen, cheerily humming to no one in particular. And the only other living thing in the whole place was a succulent that was half-dead and apparently just about to lose the will to go on.

What the hell had happened to me? That fateful morning, something just switched off. Or maybe it was the other way around—something that had been switched off for a long time had finally just switched back on. That day after my birthday, I realized I wanted more than a pile of dirty laundry and a fancy, stressful job that paid well. I wanted a more meaningful life. And it wasn't like I didn't believe my perfect sweater existed; it was more like, how long was I going to keep looking in the same sale bin over and over again?

I looked out my window at the street outside, and I saw people everywhere. A few dogs were barking. I couldn't see a single tree from any window in my apartment, and I had to put a lot of mental effort into trying to figure out where the nearest patch of grass was. My street was calm enough, and safe, but I knew that in every direction, there were more people, nonstop traffic, buses and taxis and subway stations, and more people. I was one teeny tiny cog in the huge machine that was the island of Manhattan. There was nothing like living in a place like New York City to make you feel insignificant. Suddenly I felt disconnected. From people, from nature, and from myself.

Right then and there, I decided to make a big change.

Over the next month, I gave away all my business suits save for one, said a tearful goodbye to my coworkers, my decent apartment, and the now completely dead succulent, and hauled my books, my casual clothes, and my ass back to Oklahoma. I don't know—in hindsight, maybe it was a midlife crisis thing, in that, if I had stayed in Manhattan, I would have had one. I left the rat race and the Manhattan sweater—I mean dating—scene, and took off for the prairie.

I landed in Oklahoma City, where my parents lived. I stayed with them as their houseguest, sleeping in my old room. It was like being in high school again, and I almost had to sneak out the window a few times, just like old times, to avoid getting a million questions about where I was going and instructions to be sure I took my can of mace and to "be careful out there because you never know." I had been considering staying nearby, in case they needed me as they got older. But after being unpacked for about ten minutes, I decided that it would be a very bad idea to live too close. Maybe even the same city would be a bad idea. Possibly being anywhere within a three-state radius might also be inadvisable. They meant well, but good lord, could any two people be more disappointed in my love life? Subtlety just wasn't their strong suit. They had wanted to see me married, with kids and a nice husband and a dog and a lifestyle blog. They rarely missed an opportunity to let me know I was letting them down. My older sister, Emily, had all of the things, and my parents were happy about it, but they wanted me to be the same as her. And the older I got, the more I just didn't want to fit into that mold, or any mold for that matter. Bless their hearts, they just didn't get it. And when I gave up my publishing job in New York, they thought I had completely lost my mind, so much so that before I had even moved back, they had already offered to pay for counseling. I was tempted to take the money and spend it on booze, but I thought that might be proving them right. But, if I had lived with them much longer in their house, I definitely would have been driven to drink.

I politely declined their offer for therapy and blind-date setups and immediately began looking for someplace farther away to live. After a few visits to Guthrie, I had fallen in love.

I moved to town with a decent amount of savings, and I thought about buying a house right away but ended up renting until I could figure out the lay of the land a little better and decide exactly what part of town I wanted to be in. I found a nice little house, in a quiet neighborhood, with large stately trees lining the streets. My house had two bedrooms—one for me and one for an office/guest bedroom. There was already a small garden along the side of the house and enough space in the back for a decent-sized chicken coop. Right after I signed the lease, I started looking at coop plans and found a contractor who would build one for me—even before I bought new bath towels. It's important to have one's priorities straight.

For some reason, I had thought that owning chickens would be romantic, in the way you'd expect someone from a big city to fall for the idea of animal husbandry. After living off overpriced produce and prepared foods from corner delis in Manhattan, I had been beyond excited by the idea of walking out into my own yard and grabbing the ingredients for an omelet. And while things hadn't quite turned out to be that simple, I still loved my chickens and wouldn't trade any of it. Well, except maybe for Beryl.

Once I was settled into my house, I got started on the "work" part of my new life. I leased a small retail space in one of those old brick buildings downtown and opened a bookstore, which I named "The Book Store." I know, I know. Not so original for someone who's in the writing business. But I'd had to come up with something right quick in order to pounce on a sweet lease deal. I hadn't come up with a name yet when it came time to sign the papers, so when my attorney handed me a contract that just said "Book Store" on it, I took it as a sign. At least when you saw the name of my store, you knew what I sold. I figured I could always change the name later, if I really wanted to. But I still hadn't come up with anything better. Or more accurately, I couldn't be bothered with it.

I took my name based on a sign, and then I turned the name into an actual sign and placed it in the window of my shop. I hooked up with a few book distributors, ordered fixtures, and set to work opening my store. However, the shop almost didn't open due to some drama with Leona, my straight-shootin' landlady. It was touch and go for a while there. After we signed the lease, she had somehow come to mistakenly believe that I was opening a porn shop instead of a book shop, and she and her old-timey pals thought they could scare me out of opening by secretly vandalizing my storefront and threatening to tell the sheriff I was a pornographer. I had to do a little sleuthing to catch her in the act of vandalizing her own building, but I finally did, and my attorney and I confronted her with the evidence. I managed to convince her I would not in fact be selling porn (steamy romances notwithstanding). Fortunately, at the last minute, everything got cleared up, and we reluctantly agreed that we would try to work together. I agreed not to sue her, and she agreed not to slander me in public anymore. And voilà, the store opened up. She still called or stopped by unannounced on a regular basis. She would probably never be completely convinced I was not a pornographer.

Opening the store had been harder than I'd anticipated, but I'd managed to make it work. It was kind of ironic, though: instead of being single and working long hours in New York, now I was single and working long hours in Guthrie. It was a very different type of work, to be fair—the new kind included wearing chicken-poop-covered jeans from time to time. That age-old adage seemed to apply: you could change locations, but you still brought the same baggage with you wherever you went. Moving back had proved harder than I thought it would be, between getting everything up and running and trying to work my way into the community. But I was in Guthrie to stay, and despite my mom continuing to believe I had gone bonkers and lost all ability to think reasonably, I knew deep down that it was the best decision I'd ever made in my life.

As I walked up to my bookstore and unlocked the front door, I remembered why I had moved back. And then I asked myself that other question that came up from time to time: why hadn't I moved back sooner?

TWO

MONDAY MORNINGS WERE USUALLY slow at The Book Store, so it ended up being okay that I was a little bit late in opening up. I took care of some light bookkeeping and basic housekeeping activities, like dusting the self-help section. It was tough being the owner and only full-time employee; I had to be there almost all the time. Early on I had hired one part-time employee, Julie. She was a junior over at the high school, and would sometimes cover for me for an afternoon or every other Saturday. But most of the time it was just me, with all the books, and sometimes some customers.

When I was done dusting, I decided to work on my novel, so I sat down behind the counter and pulled out my novel-outline notepad. I usually tried to write when the store was empty and I was all caught up on everything else. My pen was poised over my notepad... and I drew some big circles and started coloring them in. This repetitive motion helped me think, I reasoned. I looked up and noticed a book on the front display table was ever so slightly askew. Oh dear. I really should take every book off the table and restack them properly. This would take me through to lunchtime. Darn, no time for novel writing after all. No one was coming in the door, so I deconstructed the table.

Ever since I opened, I knew it would take some time for customers to find out about me and come in to check out the shop. More importantly, I knew it would take time for me to be accepted in the community. Even though I was an Oklahoman, I didn't grow up in Guthrie, and I'd been out of state for half my life. Small towns were close-knit and protective of their own. But there was a good mix of people in town, and if you looked closely, there were small movements occurring that might eventually lead to bigger shifts. For example, there was a growing art community, including a quilt shop, a yarn shop, and several galleries, all of which had banded together to create a monthly "art crawl" through the downtown area. There was even a new hipster coffee shop on Division Street. Which was a very good thing, because there was no way I could live somewhere that didn't have a decent coffee shop. Again, priorities.

New college grads had begun to move in (hence the hipster coffee shop), and even some young families. They added a vibrancy to the city. There was something in the air that, according to the older locals, had been missing for a long time. The old folks still weren't sure they liked the new vibrancy, however, but at least they admitted it was there. As for that "something" in the air, even though they were secretly pleased, in public they grumbled about it a lot and complained that it smelled kind of funny and not as good as it did way back in '65 when everything smelled perfect.

Just about everyone was polite, and many residents had already started shopping in my store, despite the kerfluffle that had been created by Leona. But I still needed to be patient and let my business grow organically.

One big reason people still shopped in brick-and-mortar stores in communities like Guthrie was because they wanted the social connection of being able to talk to the person behind the counter and to live in the same community as the shop owner. And because of my perceived outsider status, I knew I would have to work a little harder to become part of the town. Everyone was used to doing things a certain way, and here I was, with big-city ideas and a fancy car (it wasn't a truck) and they thought I was there to shake things up. Which, I guess I was, but I wanted it to be in a good way. I wanted to make a positive change on the local economy and the community. I idealistically wanted to make readers out of everyone (as far as ideals go, there were far worse ones out there; I thought mine was pretty legit). But it would definitely take some time for me to work my magic on Guthrie. I was prepared to wait and had figured all of this into my budget when I'd planned for the store.

Another part of my plan was to write my first novel once the shop was open. I would work on my writing in the downtime between customers and at home in the evenings. I had never attempted to write a book when I was working in publishing. I guess all my energy was spent trying to sell other people's stories. But now, I wanted to tell my own stories. I was going to write a romance novel. Or maybe a chick lit novel. Or women's fiction. I wasn't sure yet. I still hadn't gotten all that far on the project.

It turned out that the day-to-day reality of living in a small town had panned out a little differently than I'd first expected. I had really truly planned to use all the quiet time to work on my writing. Honest I had. I had figured that without the distraction of New York City and my sixty-hour-per-week editing job, I would have plenty of time to write. But nope. It turned out that my relocation to Oklahoma allowed me to rediscover a very powerful skill, one that had lain dormant until I'd moved to a town with a slower pace of life. It turned out that I was one of the absolute best procrastinators. Ever. In the history of the world. I hadn't even come up with the start of an outline for a novel yet. But I did have a yellow legal pad that had some awesome doodles on it. I was going to get to it. Maybe next week.

Around noon, I finished my deconstruction project by placing the original misaligned book back on the table, and then my stomach growled. I looked at the time on my phone —my stomach was a great lunchtime alarm clock. Time to head over to Stacy's Place.

My best friend, Kelly Passicheck, met me for lunch at Stacy's every Monday. As I walked the few blocks to the restaurant, my hair whipped in front of my face yet again, and I made another mental note that I really needed to invest in a hat or something because this wind was ridiculous. A few people waved to me out of occupied storefronts, and I waved back, happy for the acknowledgment. As I passed the chocolate shop, the door opened and someone walked out, carrying with them some really amazing chocolatey scents. My stomach grumbled its approval. I was definitely ready for lunch.

Stacy's Place was the perfect lunch spot, and Kelly and I weren't the only ones who made it our regular meeting place. You could see who was meeting with whom and check out the tourists (yes, Guthrie had tourists), all while having a delicious down-home cooked meal. I had a real soft spot for the chicken salad sandwich, with its mound of mayo-infused chicken, celery, and grapes served between two slices of perfectly toasted sprouted grain bread. Heaven.

I arrived ten minutes early, as I always did. Fortunately, I always took something to read everywhere I went, so I had something to do while I waited. Our regular waitress, Bonnie, had two iced teas already on the table, along with two menus. Damn, she was good.

Kelly spotted me sitting at our regular booth as soon as she walked in the door. She made her way across the crowded restaurant and slid into the seat across from me. Then she dumped a big pile of manila folders onto the side of the table, a slight frown furrowing her brow. I noticed that each folder had a rubber band around it to keep the contents from falling out everywhere.

"You know they have these things now called briefcases," I said nonchalantly, quickly looking back to my book. I could almost hear her scowl becoming deeper. I had made a mistake and momentarily forgot that she abhorred briefcases; it was part of her campaign to be more of a "people's attorney." I guess you had to be messy to be accessible. In any case, I decided on the spot to buy her a book bag for Christmas. It was worth a try.

Kelly was the only female attorney in Guthrie who owned her own practice. For that matter, she was also the only practicing female attorney in Guthrie. As such, she had a lot of women as clients who were very often quite bitter, because they were wanting divorces from their cheating/un-appreciative/workaholic husbands. She was the go-to attorney for women in town who needed any kind of legal help. She was unfussy, approachable, hopelessly fair, and always willing to represent the underdog. Which basically meant she was incredibly busy yet still drove an unimpressive car. When I needed help with the contract for the bookstore, and then with threatening legal action against Leona, she had proven to be a tenacious and knowledgeable attorney, who then ended up being a good friend with a quick, dry sense of humor. We discovered we had a lot in common, and I was so happy to have a friend like her.

I closed my book and put it in my bag. "So what's new?" I hoped that a quick subject change would unfurrow her brow, although I was doubtful.

"Oh, not much," she answered, taking out her reading glasses. She put them on and started looking over the menu in front of her. "Huge caseload. Corrupt legal system. Women being overpowered and manipulated by the patriarchy. You know, just the usual bullshit."

"Ah. Well." What could I say to that? "So what are you ordering today?"

She looked at me over the top of her readers and tried to look serious but ended up grinning because I was wiggling my eyebrows at her in anticipation of her answer. She sighed and closed the menu, taking her glasses back off. "Oh, I guess I'll just have my usual."

I waved at Bonnie and gave her a quick signal to indicate we would both be having our usuals. The signal consisted of me pointing at Kelly, then at myself, and ending with a shrug. Bonnie nodded and walked to the kitchen to put in our orders: one chicken salad sandwich and one fried chicken plate. It was a true wonder of the universe that Kelly was as healthy as she was, considering the way she ate.

"What's new with you?" she asked me, checking her phone and apparently not finding anything of interest on it, because she immediately tossed it onto the stack of folders and leaned back into the seat.

"The chickens got out again this morning," I answered sheepishly. Or maybe that was chickenishly.

"I told you not to get chickens, Beverley," she admonished. She had that tone in her voice. You know the one. People like to use it when you admit to a mistake they knew you were going to make.

"Bah!" I waved my hand at her with an air of carelessness. "They're great. Pretty soon they'll calm down, and then you'll see. I'll be selling eggs as well as books." So far they hadn't even produced enough for me to get a few omelets a week out of them, but I knew it was just a matter of time. They just weren't feeling at home yet. We hadn't quite fully bonded. It was all Beryl's fault.

"Okay then, good luck with that." Kelly shrugged, and I could tell she was dropping the subject but was also clearly taking great pleasure in being proved right in her belief that chickens were just no darned good. Except if they were fried, put on a dinner plate, and served with some mashed potatoes and gravy.

We made some small talk about the weather, Kelly's never-ending caseload, and the nonexistent outline for my nonexistent novel. I asked how her husband, Ben, was doing, and she answered, as she usually did, that he was fine and "still along for the ride."

Bonnie appeared with two gigantic plates of food and set them down in front of us. I had to admit that Kelly's fried chicken smelled delicious. I could also hear my arteries clogging as I inhaled. We started eating and fell silent for a while. As our face-stuffing pace slowed, the conversation picked up again and Kelly asked about the bookstore and which books were selling the best. The Book Store had both fiction and nonfiction titles, and depending on what was popular at any given time, both sold well. But overall, Guthrie seemed to be a fiction kind of town. Women's fiction sold well, as did crime fiction and mysteries.

"What's women's fiction exactly?" she asked as she worked through her obligatory scoop of green beans.

"Oh, you know, books with female lead characters, written for females. It's kind of a vague heading, really. There are all kinds of subgenres that fall under women's fiction." I could feel myself getting excited as I started talking about books. I could spend a lot of time talking about books.

"What's a subgenre?" she asked, looking at me. She could tell I liked talking about books and never minded humoring me.

"You're kidding, right?" I pointed my fork at her, then remembered that this was probably really impolite. I pointed my fork toward the ceiling instead and silently thanked her for asking me more questions about books.

"Yes. But seriously, what kinds of things fall under women's fiction? It does seem sort of broad, pardon the pun."

I snorted. "Well, romance, chick lit, erotica, to name a few. Then there are subgenres under romance—contemporary, historical, Regency, paranormal, time travel... I could go on, but I want to finish my sandwich." I could talk a long time about women's fiction in particular; it's what I had specialized in when I worked in publishing in in New York.

"Do you carry all those in your store?"

"No," I answered. "I don't have enough space. I try to carry a little bit of everything, but I'm still trying to figure out what sells best."

Kelly hunkered down in her seat and lowered her voice. "So has anyone come in asking for any, you know... weird stuff?"

I almost spit out my iced tea at her as I started laughing. "Maybe," I said just as quietly. "But that is covered by bookseller–reader confidentiality." I took another bite of my delicious sandwich. "But just for kicks, go ahead and do an internet search on dinosaur erotica later and see what comes up."

This time it was Kelly who almost sprayed iced tea across the table. "Uh, okay..."

We sat in silence for a few more bites, Kelly looking thoughtful. "What about Bigfoot?" she asked casually.

"Say what now?" I looked at her over the last half of my sandwich.

"Is there Bigfoot erotica?"

My sandwich fell out of my hand, landing back on my plate. A grape fell out of it, then rolled across the table and onto the floor.

"Excuse me?" I said, wide-eyed.

Kelly sighed, like I was the biggest idiot ever.

"I guess," I said slowly, "I could do a search on that and let you know." I knew as I said it I had no actual plans to do it.

"We have them around here, you know. Have you seen one yet?" she asked, wiping the grease off her fingers and looking around the booth, probably for more fried chicken.

"Wait. You're asking me if I've seen an erotic Bigfoot?" I just couldn't comprehend what she was trying to ask me. My mind kept trying to translate this line of conversation into something to do with shoe shopping.

"No, just a regular Bigfoot. Well, actually, I don't know how erotic they are. But—oh Christ, this is getting weird."

"Really," I smirked.

"We've got Sasquatches around here. I thought you knew that. Haven't you had a sighting yet?"

"What do you mean 'have I had a sighting yet?'" My brain was still not connecting all the dots. They were weird, scary dots.

Kelly sighed again, this time with a dramatic drop of her shoulders that indicated she was losing patience with me, and fast.

"Seriously, what the hell kind of question is that, 'have I had a sighting yet?'" I could feel my palms getting clammy and a slight sweat breaking out on my forehead. "Do they buy a lot of books or something? Is there a Sasquatch trailer park nearby? Why on earth would I see a Bigfoot?" This was definitely new territory for me. It was as if someone had suddenly thrown down a speed bump in the middle of a parking lot that I usually took at forty miles per hour. My teeth slammed together, and I started to worry about what might have just happened to my suspension.

Kelly scooped up the last of her mashed potatoes and dredged them through her cup of extra gravy. "Dinosaur, Bigfoot, it wasn't that big of a stretch. It just got me thinking about it. You're bound to see one eventually. It's just a matter of time before everyone around here calls in a Bigfoot sighting."

"To whom, the Justice League of America?"

"No, to the sheriff. Hey, I'm serious! It's a thing, you know. It's gonna happen."

I leaned back and laughed. "Yeah, I don't think so. Not to *this* Guthrie resident."

"Uh-huh," Kelly said with that tone. The one that was just waiting to prove me wrong. Well, it wasn't going to happen.

"Have you seen one?" I asked her.

"Yup!" she said proudly, sitting up straight. "Well, sort of. Maybe."

I wasn't letting her off easy, mostly because it was just such blatant bullshit. "You either have, or you haven't. Like inhaling. Or sex."

She looked confused for a minute as she tried to follow my logic. She finally gave up trying to form an argument. "Okay, fine, I've never actually seen one. But I've talked to lots of people who have. People you wouldn't think believe in it, either, but they've really seen one. So... the evidence is compelling."

I was surprised by this. Kelly was a logical, rational woman. "Come on, that's just ridiculous. I don't believe you. There's no such thing! Sasquatch is a hoax; it's been disproved like a billion different times."

She raised an eyebrow at me.

"Oh *please!*" I said. I could feel myself getting really agitated, but I wasn't exactly sure why. Maybe because the conversation was so incredibly stupid. "Anyone who believes in that hooey is certifiably crazy. Or just plain stupid."

"You may want to rethink that, Bev," she said, leaning forward and reaching for the check. "If we had to commit everyone in town who believed in Bigfoot, no one would be left. And I happen to have a very high IQ, thank you very much. I'm telling you—it's just a matter of time before you see him. Or her. Or whatever. Your house is a little further outside of town—a lot of sightings happen out that way."

I was speechless. But only for a few seconds because then the questions came fast and furious. I started bouncing my left leg around under the table as a way to vent my mounting anxiety. A rivulet of sweat trickled down my back. "How on earth do you know where most Bigfoot sightings occur in Guthrie? And why on earth do you actually care?"

"I don't know. Call it a hobby, I guess." She could tell she was making me nervous, and I could tell she was loving it. "Why, are you *scared* of Bigfoot, Bev?" Her eyebrows raised.

As a reply to her question, I thought about running out of the restaurant screaming in terror and heading in the general direction of Texas. Instead, I resisted the urge to flee the state and kept sitting in my Naugahyde seat. "Nah," I said in a voice that wouldn't have even fooled a five-year-old. "I just think they're stupid." I took my napkin and wiped my forehead.

"Relax," she said calmly. "I mean, it's not like one has ever killed anyone or anything. That we know of, anyway." My jaw dropped and my leg stopped bouncing. A small smile showed at the corner of her mouth as she picked up her phone to check the time. "Oh shit, I've got to run. I'll catch up with you later," she said as she tossed some money on the table, picked up all her files, and left the restaurant, leaving me sitting there wondering what had just happened. Bigfoot? In my backyard? Yeah, not so much.

I said goodbye to Bonnie after settling the bill and left the restaurant. I stood outside for a minute, still considering making a run toward Texas. I tried to get the image of a big hairy monster killing people out of my head. The idea that Bigfoot actually existed terrified me. Like, a level-ten type of terrified. The kind of terrified that sends people into therapy for five years. I took three deep breaths and started walking. There was just no way that they could be real. No way. I didn't care what my best friend said. She could be the best feminist lawyer in the world, but she was apparently full of horse poop.

I walked back toward the shop, admiring the tops of the old buildings across the street, with their ornate window trim and fancy brick- and stonework. One building had the year 1904 embedded on a date stone above the entrance. I wondered what the building originally housed way back then.

The shadows had gotten a little longer during my lunch break, and an almost imperceptible change in the weather had occurred over the last few hours. Somehow the air was a little different—maybe a little less humid, or the breeze came from a slightly different direction. Whatever it was, it signaled that a season change was close at hand, and it felt pretty good. But as I kept walking, it seemed as if the shift in the air was signaling some other impending change. Something more... mysterious. Or scary. I couldn't quite put my finger on it. Maybe it was all the Bigfoot talk. Or maybe it was simply that I hadn't been back home long enough to be familiar with all these subtle changes. Yeah, that was probably it.

THREE

EVERY MONDAY AFTERNOON I took an extra-long lunch hour so that I could attend the staff meeting for the *Guthrie Ledger*, the local paper. Because on top of raising chickens, running The Book Store, and settling into my new town, I had decided to find a part-time job.

To help out with covering my sundry home and business expenses (and probably to avoid writing my book), I had taken a gig with the *Ledger* not long after I'd moved to town. Even though I'd never been a reporter before, Mark Ellison, the managing editor, was so excited to have a big-time New York book nerd on his staff that he'd hired me before I even came in to check out the offices. It didn't hurt that we had gone to school together in OKC and that he'd had a huge crush on me in eighth grade. But those crushes fade as quickly as ice cream melts on the summer sunbaked sidewalk, and we had gone our separate ways after high school. He'd gone to Kansas University to study journalism, I'd gone off to New York, and we'd lost touch until I checked out the *Ledger* masthead and discovered he had settled in my new hometown. It turned out that he'd taken a job in Guthrie right out of college and had been there ever since. He probably wanted to be near—but not too close—to his parents, just like me. Smart guy.

The best part of working at the paper wasn't the tiny salary, but rather the social aspect of the job. It turned out to be a good way to meet people all over town, and it was an even better way for them to get to know me. I could tell pretty early on that it would take some work to shed my outsider status in Guthrie, and working at the paper was a darn good start. And it turned out that I loved writing news articles. I'd had one or two journalism classes in college but hadn't done any real nonfiction writing since then, save for editorial comments and such. Now that I was at the *Ledger*, I could hone my skills. It was a nice complement to writing fiction, or at least it would be—if I were writing any fiction.

Writing for the paper was also a chance to sneak in a few more positive aspects into the news landscape which, let's face it, could be a pretty grim place sometimes. I liked to call my ploy *Subversive Optimism*. Yeah, I'd totally watch that reality show.

This afternoon I arrived at the Guthrie *Ledger* offices only a few minutes late, having stopped at Hoboken Coffee for a cappuccino to go. Cappuccinos were my secret weapon against involuntary napping during *Ledger* staff meetings.

I walked into the conference room prepared with a fake excuse for my tardiness—something about having just come from an interview for Something Very Important. But it turned out an excuse wasn't necessary, because Mark hadn't even come in yet.

A few other employees had already arrived (not that there were many of us to begin with), and Grace, the assistant editor, was sitting at the head of the table. All of us knew—including Grace—that she would have to switch seats when Mark got there, but she liked to imagine she was the managing editor. So we all let her. I mean, there didn't seem to be any harm in it.

Grace once mentioned that she believed in the law of attraction. I didn't know much about it myself, but I knew it had something to do with the premise that like attracts like. I felt that Grace might have a flawed understanding of the basic principles, though. She seemed to believe in imagining she already had what she wanted. Which was fine, as far as I could see, as long as no one got hurt. But then she would complain when what she wanted didn't actually show up. She would always talk about her "boyfriend" when we all knew she didn't really have one, and wasn't likely to attract one, especially if she kept cavorting around town holding hands with an imaginary man—no matter how handsome he was purported to be. But to paraphrase one of my favorite aphorisms, to each her own imaginary boyfriend.

As soon as I parked myself in a chair and took on an air of being bored from having been there for ages, Mark walked into the room in his usual huff. Suddenly everyone was sitting up a little taller, with their pencils poised at the ready over their notebooks. He looked at Grace sitting in his chair, and she sighed heavily before scooting over one seat. He strode across the room, and I admired him as he did so. He had been good-looking way back when, and he was one of those men who was aging well. His espresso-brown hair had a few flecks of gray in it now, but it suited him. His dark eyes were often guarded but alluring. Almost sultry... Ach! I needed to snap out of it. I just needed more coffee, I told myself, as I took a big sip from my to-go cup.

"Sorry I'm late, everyone," Mark said as he sat down heavily in his chair. "The ad department seems to have their heads stuck up their collective ass again." He carelessly tossed a stack of papers onto the table, and they slid all over the place. This was his way of passing out copies to everyone. He wasn't known for being much of a hand-holder, or even for being very pleasant, for that matter. Apparently manners and a congenial personality didn't get you very far in the newspaper business. This seemed to be the polar opposite of the publishing business, I noted. I made a split-second decision to never go into newspaper editing. It seemed that a long, contentious divorce could really wreak havoc on your ability to be happy or even just plain nice to people. Poor guy. Still, he was old enough to know better. But he was the boss, so the rest of us were all just along for the ride.

"John, what's the deal on the article about the latest proposal for the State Capital Company Building?" And with that, Mark started his no-fuss, no-muss rundown of outstanding articles. Once he had grilled everyone about their current assignments, he started handing out new ones. Jade got a story about the new candle shop opening at the corner of Oklahoma and Broad, Grace was assigned to the next meeting of the Guthrie Quilting Guild, and Burns got a story about hard times that had befallen a local chicken farmer. Damn, some people got all the luck. I was starting to wonder if I had been left out of the next round, but then Mark turned to me.

"Beverley, Al Turner called in a Bigfoot sighting to the sheriff's office yesterday. It's the second call in a week. I want you to go talk to him. And talk to Leona Tisdale, too. She says Bigfoot was rooting through her trash last Friday. It's actually been a while since we've run a major Bigfoot story, so go ahead and put together a comprehensive piece."

"Wait, did you just say 'Bigfoot'?" I asked, trying to sound casual but realizing it may have come out sounding more panic-stricken than carefree. I hoped my eyes didn't have that spirally, crazy look they sometimes got when I was anxious. "You mean, like, Sasquatch Bigfoot?"

Mark exhaled a forceful breath and threw his pencil on the table. "What other Bigfoot is there, Bev? You New Yorkers got something fancier up East?" This last remark elicited a smirk from several of my fellow employees, who hadn't exactly warmed up to the idea of having one of those fancy New Yorkers in their midst yet, even if she was originally an Okie from way back when. Because taking off for the big city years ago meant I was no longer a local, plain and simple. And I couldn't figure out what it would take to regain that status. Questioning the existence of Bigfoot didn't seem to me to be the way to do it, though. I was still at square one with these people, and Mark knew just how to push my buttons.

"It's the same Bigfoot up East, presumably," I began, sounding factual. "The same, imaginary, fake Bigfoot."

Mark pointed his finger at me in protest and opened his mouth to speak, but I cut him off.

"Mark! Everyone knows that Bigfoot isn't real. You really want me to try and do a serious news story on a fictional character?" I laughed, or scoffed really, like there was no way this guy could be expecting me to actually do this assignment. "Nobody is going to go for something like that."

"Beverley!" he shot back at me. "Everyone will go for something like that. Bigfoot is not fictional. Go get me a story. A real story. Show us small-town folks how it's done." Snark

Alert! Clearly his crush on me from eighth grade was no longer winning me any brownie points. He got up and picked up his stack of papers and his pencil, which had landed on the other side of the table when he'd thrown it. Then he stalked out the door, leaving me with no choice but to look each remaining person in the eye, trying to confirm with them that I was really supposed to go write a news story about a made-up monster.

But no one met my pleading, crazy-person gaze; everyone looked down at their notepads, writing their quick pretend notes and avoiding my eyes. Then they all shuffled out of the room one by one, without so much as a conciliatory "good luck with that, Bev."

I sat there by myself for a few minutes, unable to move, feeling like I had the plague. Or like I was an alien from the Rational Galaxy who had just crash landed on Planet What the Hell. This just couldn't be. I started to feel clammy again. I took a few deep breaths, got up from my chair, and walked straight to Mark's office, where he had barricaded himself behind his two giant computer screens that were placed strategically in the middle of his desk. All I could see was the top of his head over the screens, part of a keyboard on the surface of the desk, and his coffee cup next to the keyboard. The pencil seemed to be MIA. I gently closed the door behind me. This situation called for a different approach other than actual logic.

"Maaark." I lengthened and smoothed out his name to make it sound like what I imagined maple syrup to sound like. I figured I could sweet-talk my way out of this pretend article and into a real assignment, like the one about the chicken farmer. "You're not really serious about the whole Sasquatch thing, are you?" I smiled, hoping he would peer around his computer screens to notice I was standing there batting my eyelashes at him.

But he didn't look up. "Yup, I'm serious." I heard a hint of anger in his voice and then the sound of a pencil being placed loudly on the surface of the desk. I could tell by the sound that it was a pencil, and not a pen. He slammed it down so hard that I was sure the lead had shattered inside its wooden protective cover. He finally leaned his head to the side and gave me a look that singed my once-flittering eyelashes. I started to think that maybe this hadn't been such a good idea after all. He stood up now, rising to his full six feet and putting his hands on his hips in a defensive posture. "Look, just go write it, okay? What's the big deal? You haven't had a problem with any of your other assignments."

"Yeah, but you've always given me actual news stories to write. This isn't news, it's..."

"Of course it's news. At least, to the people around here it is. We do things differently in Guthrie, not like you uppity urban New York hipsters. If a few people saw Bigfoot over the weekend, then it's a story. End of story."

"First off, this is just not news!" I protested.

"And?"

"And I'm not an urban hipster!" I snapped. "If you'd do your research, you'd know that the age demographic for the cultural term hipster—"

This time it was his turn to cut me off.

"Well, if it's not news, then what the hell is it?" He was getting thoroughly mad at me. I watched for steam coming out of his ears.

"—but there is some disagreement as to the exact start date of the Millennial era—"

"Goddamnit, Bev," Mark said quietly. Uh-oh.

I spewed the truth all over his desk. "Well, it just isn't actual news. It's fake news. It's ridiculous is what it is."

"Beverley. Just go write the goddamned story already."

"Yeah, but..." My voice trailed off.

"But what? Look, I don't have time for this. What? What is it already?" he pleaded with me, mostly so that he could just get me out of his office.

"Can I maybe trade stories with someone?" I tried the syrup approach again. "Maybe I could switch with someone who, um, has more experience with Bigfoot?"

Mark walked around his desk now and placed his hand on my shoulder. My skin grew a little warmer, and I could feel myself relaxing a little bit. Until I realized that he was simply trying the maple syrup approach on *me* now and trying to shove me out the door of his office, which he had opened without me noticing in the midst of my touch-induced relaxation response.

"I think you're the perfect man for the job, Green," he said with one final push to my shoulder. "Go get 'em." I stumbled across the threshold and heard the door slam shut behind me before I could even turn around and ask him what the heck I was supposed to go get exactly, and before I could yell at him for calling me a man. I was pretty sure he knew I wasn't actually a man, so what had he meant by that?

Oh. I suddenly got it. He wanted me to grow a pair. What a tool! No wonder his ex-wife divorced him. I made a mental note to let the air out of his tires on my way back to my shop. So much for the syrup approach. That rat bastard.

FOUR

BACK AT THE BOOKSTORE, I sat behind the counter and waited for the crowds to roll in. And by crowds I meant Myrna and Justin Miller, who would come in every Monday afternoon to pick out one new book each—he would buy a Western or a US history book; she would get a romance novel. They were late. Not that I was paying attention that closely or anything.

I knew from the start that it would take time for my business to get established and for sales to pick up. My rational business mind knew that I would have to work hard at gaining people's trust and friendship, and until that happened, I needed to be patient. Things would be slow and I'd need to sit tight, and eventually, business would increase. I had accounted for all this when I'd created my budget for the bookstore, but that didn't keep me from being impatient sometimes when my cash register went too long without seeing any action. I could go long periods of time without seeing any action, but I really wanted my cash register to get some.

I sat in the quiet, empty shop and asked myself that question again. The one about why I moved here. No answer came through the door. I took a deep breath and reminded myself once again to be patient. I could always spend my time working on my Bigfoot article. I could even write an entire series of articles about the various cryptids of the world. Starting with Sasquatch. As I recalled my impending assignment, I felt a knot form in my stomach. This article was really getting to me. I hadn't wanted to admit to myself why this was, but there was just no denying it any longer. I was just plain scared of Bigfoot—had been all my life. Some people had a fear of getting stuck in an elevator, or of being buried alive, or maybe of being eaten by a giant moth. My fear was of being captured by Bigfoot and held hostage, forced to clean his cave and make him dinner. As I got older my fears morphed to include other ungodly and unmentionable acts, like having to trim his ear hair or wash his beastly undergarments. If I'd wanted any of that, I'd be married. Which might explain why I wasn't currently married.

It was all my sister's fault. Damn Emily and her evil older-sister ways. When we were kids, she would scare the living daylights out of me by telling me that if I didn't finish my dinner, Bigfoot was going to come and eat it, and then he would eat me for dessert. We went through a phase, once she had discovered that any mention of Bigfoot made me wide-eyed and petrified, and she rode that horse into the ground. She rode that Sasquatch until it couldn't be ridden anymore. She kept adding to her arsenal of threats. It started with dinner; then it expanded to include putting away the dishes for her, folding her laundry, and bringing the mail in. I started having nightmares and insisted on sleeping with my parents.

Finally it got so bad that they had to have a serious talk with my sister and tell her to knock it off, or they'd make her get a job to pay for any visits to a counseling professional I might need. Even though she was only ten.

She finally stopped once she got bored with it, but not before a permanent fear of all things relating to Bigfoot had etched itself on my brain.

Yup, just thinking about Bigfoot now gave me a big old case of the heebie-jeebies, and I'd just as soon go back to not thinking about it. I'd managed to do so for very large parts of my life, after all. But here I was, now having to write an article about my biggest fear and interview people who believed my fear existed. I would have to do "research" about a scary monster. I could feel a cold sweat breaking out across my forehead yet again. Did I really move back to Oklahoma to write "news articles" like this one?

"Hello, Beverley," I heard a voice say right in front of me. I had been so lost in thought that I hadn't even noticed Myrna and Justin coming in.

"Oh hi, Myrna, how's things?"

"Pretty good, pretty good!" Myrna chirped. She was a small woman with delicate features and a long, curved nose. She smiled a lot, and when she spoke, it really was as if she was chirping. I always expected her to take flight every time she left the store. "Say," she went on, "could you help me pick out a book for my grandson this week? He loves tractors."

"Sure thing!" I said brightly, springing up from my stool. I was glad for the business and glad for the distraction. Because dredging up all this stuff from my childhood was not going to get me anywhere.

I helped Myrna and Justin find some books, and as they

came up to the register to pay, I decided to take their pulse on the whole Bigfoot thing.

"Hey, Justin, you don't happen to believe in Bigfoot, do you?" I watched his face as I asked the question. I expected him to laugh or look surprised, but he didn't even bat an eye.

"Oh yes," he said earnestly, running his fingers through his fine mousy-brown hair. "Absolutely."

"Have you, uh, ever seen one?" I figured I might as well go all the way.

"No, I've never seen one, but my dad saw one, way back in the day, and my granddad used to tell all kinds of stories about Bigfoot encounters." Myrna stood by him, nodding her head in agreement.

Until today, I had taken them for rational people. Damnit. Well, as long as they kept buying books, I didn't necessarily have to think they were sane.

"I see," I said slowly. "Interesting."

"Why?" Justin said in a squeaky voice. "Have you seen one?" Myrna perked up and watched me expectantly.

"No, of course not!" I declared loudly.

"Oh," said Myrna, sounding very disappointed.

"I'm writing an article on Bigfoot for the paper," I explained. "Just trying to do some, uh, research."

"You do believe in Bigfoot, don't you?" Justin asked, cocking his head at me.

How could I answer this without really answering? Normally I'd just shout "oh *hell* no!" but I kind of wanted to keep the Millers as customers. It was a fine line in a small town—you had to leave room for all points of view in life, but everything you did or said ended up under a microscope. It seemed that believing in Bigfoot was up there with topics like religion and politics in Guthrie

"I'm looking into it" was all I said, smiling broadly. "Maybe I can contact you if I need any good stories?"

"Absolutely!" Justin volunteered.

I thanked him and told him I would let him know if I needed to go back as far as whenever "the day" was for my research. They paid for their books and said some very cheery, chirpy goodbyes before leaving the shop.

I was sad to see them go as they closed the door behind them. I needed another distraction, right away. Reminiscing about my childhood and the origins of my Sasquatch fear was counterproductive. So I tried to make my brain banish the subject and opted for manual labor instead.

I decided to make myself useful and unpack a few boxes that the UPS guy had left at the door while I was out to lunch. I made a mental note to ask him, once more, to please not leave boxes outside my shop when I wasn't there. Never mind that everyone in this town knew everyone else, and there was virtually no crime—I was still paranoid. I had lived in New York City, damnit, where I learned really fast that you couldn't leave so much as a used plastic fork unattended for twenty seconds without it getting nicked. "Don't trust who you don't know" had been my basic motto for over twenty years, and it was a hard habit to break. You just never knew, you know? And with a landlady who wasn't above vandalizing her own property, I didn't think it was a good idea to leave my porn stash—I mean books—unattended outside.

Also, the UPS guy was ruggedly good-looking in a muscly, box-lifting kind of way, and I didn't like it when I missed his visits. I could picture him on the cover of a romance novel, his brown shirt unbuttoned to his navel, one hand resting on a hand truck stacked with boxes and a windswept blonde woman sitting on top of the boxes. I thought of a funny "I'll sign for your package anytime" line and decided to use it in my book.

But even thinking about the UPS guy wasn't working. I still felt put out about that dumb newspaper assignment. My mind wandered once again, and I reached for my novel-writing notebook and made some scribbles about a possible book plot. *I Married Bigfoot*, I scrawled on a fresh page. It could be a romance, or it could be a thriller. Or if this article really went south, maybe it could be a true crime or current affairs book. But I couldn't really think of anything specific to write about yet, so instead I just drew about two hundred little circles all around what I'd just written. This way, the page wouldn't look so empty. I felt satisfied.

After my hand began to cramp up from all the circle drawing, I stared out the front windows of the store and sighed loudly and forlornly. Nope, it wasn't computing. Just because I had an irrational fear of Bigfoot that may be causing me to freak out about the assignment a little more than someone might expect, didn't mean that having to write a serious article about a made-up monster wasn't still a really stupid idea. Nope, it definitely wasn't me. It was them. They were all crazy in this town.

Everyone—and by everyone, I meant *everyone*—knew that this stuff was all made-up, right? Sasquatch was obviously fake, nothing more than a myth, a fictional figure from old tales created to scare the living daylights out of people like me by people like my sister. I had learned to rationalize most of my fears as I got older. It worked sometimes. But still —no way was Bigfoot a real thing! Everybody had seen those "home movies" of a tall guy dressed up in a furry ape suit, the quality of the film so grainy that you couldn't tell if you were looking at a monster or a wet mop. And those crazy conspiracy theorists... I wondered if I was going to end up having to interview some of those wackos. Oh man. What had I gotten into.

FIVE

I took my time walking home once I'd closed the shop for the day. What was the rush? Yeah, I had to make sure the chickens hadn't escaped and made a run for the Kansas border, but other than that, the only thing waiting for me at home was Bigfoot.

When I walked in the front door, I dumped my bag in the kitchen and made a beeline for the backyard, where I fed the chickens and then sat on the patio.

I couldn't help but think this was all Kelly's fault. Why had she asked me at lunch, right out of the blue, about seeing Bigfoot? That had been way too weird to be a coincidence. Yep, it was all her fault. And even though I was mad at her for manifesting this stupid article into existence, she was also still the only person I could think of to call and vent to. I pulled my phone out of my back pocket and dialed her number.

"Damn you and your freakishly accurate clairvoyant skills!" It wasn't how I usually started a phone call, but these were unusual times. The chickens stared at me nervously.

"Um, hello?" Kelly sounded confused.

"I don't even know where to start!" I practically yelled into my cell phone, after I relayed the basics of my situation to her. "What the hell!" My aggravation and time alone to think about it way too much had combined to turn me into an insolent, indignant bookstore owner/reporter.

"Well," said Kelly calmly, since she was used to my occasional anxiety-prone rants by now, "you worked in fiction for over twenty years, so this shouldn't be too much of a stretch for you, right?" I detected a noise coming over the line that could possibly have been the sound of her trying not to laugh at me.

"I don't work for the *National Enquirer* for cripes' sake. I mean, I know this is a small town, but it's a *newspaper*, and last time I checked, news articles are supposed to be factual. Except if it's about politics, in which case all bets are off. But this is supposed to be serious journalism, damnit!" I slammed my fist on the patio table. Ow.

Kelly didn't bother trying to cover up the phone at all this time as she laughed at me. "Well, then just treat this as you would any other investigative piece. Go look up what's been written before."

"You're telling me how to write a newspaper article?" I asked indignantly.

"You asked."

"Oh. Right."

"Go talk to the latest round of witnesses. Find a local expert or two."

"There are Bigfoot experts? Around *here*?" I asked. My insolence was about to turn into hysterical laughter.

"Oh sure," she said. "Remember, Bigfoot has been an

Oklahoma native for a long time. There's folks around here who know quite a bit about it all."

"Like who?" I decided then and there that I needed to meet a Bigfoot expert.

"Try Danny Cadence. He knows a lot about the local Bigfoot scene."

Danny Cadence. I made a mental note. *Bigfoot scene.* This time I was the one who had trouble stifling my laugh. "So, any idea where can I find this Mr. Cadence? Does he live in the woods somewhere with his mother and a talking pumpkin?"

"I'm not exactly sure what he's up to these days," Kelly said with a factual air, ignoring my jab. "He lives up north of town, but Mark can track him down for you; they're friends. Oh, and you should probably talk to the sheriff. He's the one who has to field all those calls."

I laughed. "I'll bet the sheriff just hangs up on all those wackos who call in with a sighting."

"I doubt it," she said. "I told you, it's a thing here."

"Yes, right. A thing. A crazy thing. This is cray-*zee!*" I just couldn't see how she was staying so rational about all this.

"Well, if you really feel that way, why don't you just write it as a fictional story? Or an exposé maybe?"

I was silent for a few seconds before answering, as I considered these angles. Picking one might be my only way to get through the assignment. It might not be great "journalism," but that may not matter so much—or less than I had hoped. "That's a possibility, I guess."

"It might not make you any friends, but at least you'd be true to your 'journalistic ethics' or whatever your deal is."

I frowned into the phone. "What do you mean it won't make me any friends?"

"Like I said, people around here take Bigfoot seriously. If you make fun of them, or try to prove them wrong, you might just stir up a hornet's nest for yourself. They won't like you."

I hadn't thought of this. Mostly because I hadn't realized that slandering Bigfoot in Guthrie would be equivalent to advocating for child labor. "For reals, Kelly. You're an attorney. You deal in well-presented arguments. Tell me you don't think this is just a little bit bat-shit crazy?"

"Not necessarily," she answered me. "The world is not black and white."

"Spoken like a true lawyer," I muttered. "Okay. Well, I appreciate your thoughts, anyway. I guess. I will take them under advisement."

"Also spoken like a true lawyer," she laughed at me. "If the newspaper fires you, you could always try to pass the bar."

"Yeah, sure. Sasquatch can be my first client." I thanked Kelly and ended the call, making a mental note to contact the sheriff and to text Mark and ask him where I could find one Danny Cadence. But later. I still couldn't believe I was going to have to do this. Maybe if I waited a little longer to get started, it would all just magically disappear.

All this mental anguish was making me hungry. I went into the kitchen but kept wandering around aimlessly because I kept forgetting why I was in there. To say I was somewhat distracted was an understatement. Bigfoot continued to take his toll on me. I had moved to Oklahoma to get away from the hustle, grind, and overall freak show that was New York. I had moved here to live a simple life—to enjoy some peace and quiet, cheap real estate, and to get some writing done without any distractions. Sasquatch was not part of my three, five, or ten year Life Plan.

When my stomach started grumbling, I remembered why I was in the kitchen. I warmed up a bowl of my homemade potato and vegetable soup and sat down with it and my reporter's notebook. I wrote down Danny's name and added "call sheriff" to my to-do list.

The way I saw it, I had three options on how to approach the story. I wrote them down so I could stare at them balefully.

- *Option 1: Write a clear, concise "news story," sticking to "the facts" from eyewitnesses and any supporting data I can find. Pros: I could keep my job and make everyone happy. Cons: I would be lying, and I'd feel like a total fraud.*

- *Option 2: Write an exposé proving everyone in town wrong, except for me. Pros: Personal vindication! Possible journalism award! Cons: I could disappoint the town, lose business at The Book Store, and possibly lose my job.*

- *Option 3: Approach it as fiction and write a combination of options 1 and 2 in such a way that readers won't be able*

to tell what they're reading, but they'll
want to keep reading it. Pros: Keep job,
make people happy, be able to live with
myself. Cons: I still have to write the
damn thing.

Staring at my options balefully didn't seem to help. I couldn't handle it. I just wanted out; it was that plain and simple. I reached for my phone and sent Mark a message under a pretext that I thought seemed plausible.

Me: *Hey—have you seen my favorite pencil anywhere?*

Mark: *no*

Me: *Also you were just kidding about writing an article on Sasquatch, right?*

Mark: *no*

All right, well, at least I was trying all the angles. But it was time to put together some kind of plan for this article. Just the thought of actually not being able to get out of it sent another wave of anxiety through me. At this point I contemplated breaking out an Emergency Beer from the fridge but went for the Emergency Cookies instead. Cookies can fix damn near everything.

I was going to have to turn something in by Sunday night, so if I was going to do this, I would need to start interviewing and researching soon. My first thought was that this would be a great time to thoroughly clean my bathroom, including regrouting the tub and installing a new sink faucet. I started to browse YouTube for tub-grouting videos. But then I stopped myself. I needed to get serious.

I continued to review my options carefully, while

munching on cookies. I thought once more about having to trim Bigfoot's nose hairs. I decided I'd go ahead and take whatever was behind Curtain Number 3. I added a few more items to my to-do list and decided to get started straightaway. Tomorrow.

SIX

I woke up slowly on Tuesday morning, rolling over onto my side and opening my eyes to the bright early-morning sunshine. It was a glorious feeling to wake up naturally, without an alarm. I felt a few seconds of peace and satisfaction. Then, without meaning to, I thought about Bigfoot. I tried not to, but there he was, in bed with me. I mean, he wasn't really in bed with me (I felt around under the covers just to be sure), but he may as well have been. I yawned, gave up on trying to kick him out, and instead invited him to breakfast. We ate in the kitchen, with very little conversation. His table manners left something to be desired.

First thing I did once the bookstore was open was call Al Turner and make arrangements to drive out to his place that afternoon for an interview. I could do it on my lunch hour since I was the boss; I simply gave myself permission to take a longer break than usual. It wasn't ideal to have the shop closed, but most everyone took a little time off in the middle of the day to eat or run a few errands. Even bookstore owners needed to do stuff like go to the dentist or perform important newspaper business.

I then tried to put together a quick list of questions for Al. It didn't take long. What was I going to ask him besides "are you nuts?" If the interview didn't stop right there, maybe I'd follow up with "seriously, are you nuts?" Forget the questions. I'd wing it.

I could have worked on my novel, but instead I ended up doing a little internet surfing. I started out looking for Sasquatch information, but that gave me a headache after about thirty seconds. So I bought a nice-looking new pair of running shoes instead. It happens.

Finally, I couldn't take it anymore. The anticipation about the interview was driving me nuts, so around noonish, I ate a quick lunch behind the counter and then closed up shop. I decided that I deserved a cappuccino from Hoboken for extra mental fortitude, so I stopped at the coffeehouse on my way out of town. The twenty-minute drive would be much more pleasant with a coffee drink to keep me company.

Hoboken was a super cute little coffee shop. It was off Division Street, the main drag, but it was hidden behind an abandoned garage, and the only sign of it from the street was a small sandwich board, about the size of a real estate "for sale" sign. You pretty much had to know the place was there —or you at least had to have searched for it on your phone. I had no idea why the owners had named it after a city in New Jersey. Someday I'd write an article about them for the paper and find out the story behind the name. But for now it remained a mystery.

The place was almost always packed. Everywhere you looked, people were drinking coffee or tea, visiting with friends, or working alone on their laptops. It was a great example of "new school meets old school" in this small town. A coffee shop like Hoboken was solidly hipster, with its austere decor, concrete countertops, and shelf full of vinyl records. And at least half the patrons were wearing skinny jeans and sporting earbuds. But Hoboken also appealed to GenXers like me who were older and sufficiently jaded, but still tech-savvy enough to need a place to get caffeinated while looking for new jobs on our laptops. And sometimes you would even see some old-timers sprinkled in the crowd, drinking black coffee and watching their grandchildren eat vegan raspberry crumble muffins. I loved coming to Hoboken and taking the pulse of my new city. Coffee brought everyone together and always made everything better.

As I waited for Seth, owner and also my favorite barista, to make my cappuccino, I noticed a man walk into the shop. I hadn't seen him before, and I wondered if this was because he wasn't a local or if he'd just had bad timing up till now. Either way, I looked him over. I sized him up. I gazed upon him like he was a NotNeutral porcelain six-ounce cappuccino cup filled to the brim with espresso and smooth, sweet steamed milk. With a chocolate almond biscotti on the side. I told myself this was okay to do because first of all, it didn't seem like anyone was noticing that I was ogling, and second of all, no one had to know that I'd just compared a man to a cappuccino and a cookie. I also reasoned that I didn't always want to be staring at my phone. So I stared at this man instead.

He was really good-looking. My jaw started to drop as I took an even closer look. I was always on the lookout for the elusive Really Good-Looking Man, but he seemed harder and harder to find. On the rare occasion I did see one, my interest was immediately piqued. Like today. Yes, men like him seemed to be rare these days. Either I was getting pickier as I got older, or men my age really weren't aging well. In which case, my choices of potential romantic partners were dwindling fast, minute by minute. If they weren't aging well, I thought, maybe I wasn't aging well, either, and who knew what they thought about me. An existential panic began to set in, and I realized that either way I was screwed. And I hadn't even got my coffee yet. I had once again achieved inner-monologue romance oblivion. Yay, me.

I tried to shake myself out of it and convince my brain to just shut up and go back to ogling. I could just admire this nice-looking person and leave it at that. Zip it, brain! Let the body have some fun.

The Really Good-Looking Man had walked farther into the shop and was now in line to order. Sometimes a man would be so good-looking that it might make you do a double-take but then run the other way, because upon closer inspection he actually seemed like a jerk or was just too handsome for his own good. But this guy was different. He was good-looking in a friendly, approachable way. He had a sort of calm, easy presence. It was very attractive all on its own. He wasn't a large person, maybe five foot nine or ten, and had a lean, well-defined figure. His hair was sandy blond and curly, and it looked a little windblown, like he'd been outside a while. I noticed that his bright blue eyes lit up the shop as he smiled and said hi to Seth. I couldn't help but smile a little, too, as I watched him. I forgot that I was trying to scope him out on the down-low. I caught myself, looked away, and hoped no one had noticed.

But I couldn't look away for very long. My gaze slowly

moved back to him, as if drawn by magnetic force. The laugh lines around his eyes made him seem friendly and open. I kept watching him as he waited, his hands in his jeans pockets, his shoulders up around his ears as he shivered once. Oooh! That almost made me shiver, too. I found myself wishing I could see his hands. I liked to think I could tell a lot about a man by his hands. And his shoes. Yep, a man's hands and shoes spoke volumes. It wasn't about the size; it was about the quality. In both cases. I had always been a "quality over quantity" advocate, and men were no exception.

My gaze continued to travel south toward his feet (noting briefly along the way how well his jeans fit) and landed on a pair of expensive boots. Expensive, but well-worn. Quality over quantity. He wasn't just talking the talk; he was also for sure walking the walk. Either I had an undiagnosed heart murmur, or he just made my chest a little fluttery.

I was still watching him as he ordered. He asked Seth for a cappuccino. Huh. Well, he was good-looking *and* he had good taste in coffee. What an appealing combination.

I must have been looking more intensely than I realized because suddenly I heard Seth calling my name in a way that sounded like it might be the third or fourth time he'd said it. The handsome stranger looked my way, and I could feel my cheeks getting red. Damnit! I was too old for this blushing crap, but it still happened when I got really flustered. I guess I was more attracted to him than I realized—I even surprised myself with my reaction.

In order to pick up my cappuccino, I had to walk up next to him. I made a split-second decision to go for it. And by go for it, I mean not ignore him like I would have if I were in line in a coffee shop in New York. Instead I gathered my five feet and five inches up as tall as I could, and as I approached the counter, I looked him in the eye and gave him a slight smile as I did so. I picked up my paper to-go cup, said thanks and bye to Seth, turned to leave, and promptly dropped my phone. It just fell right out of my hand and landed with a very loud *slap* on the concrete floor. Right at Mr. Cute Boots' boots.

Oh dear. Now I was really flustered. I started to bend down to pick up my phone, but halfway down it occurred to me that oh, this might be getting too far up into Mr. Cute Boots' personal space, so I stopped, midbend. Then I proceeded to spill my coffee. On my phone. And maybe on his boots. I was too discombobulated to check closely.

My fluster level kept rising, and quickly. I was in grave danger of completely losing my shit in a manner of seconds. Now what should I do... stand up, or continue to bend down and pick up my coffee-soaked phone? I was stuck, midstoop. In the short time it took me to think all these complicated thoughts, he had pulled some napkins from the stack on the counter and was bending down to pick up my phone. He stood up, wiping my phone off, and then I stood the rest of the way up. He extended his hand out to me, and my phone was resting on a napkin on his palm. I still had enough of my wits about me to be disappointed that I couldn't see his hand underneath it.

"Here you go," he said casually.

I could tell I was blushing even more, but I did manage to look him in the eyes again as I reached out for my phone— and almost spilled the rest of my coffee. Could this get any worse?

Up close, I was able to get a much better look at his clear blue eyes. He had X-ray eyes. They were that kind of blue that zapped you right down to your bones and in the process read every single thought in your brain, especially the dirty ones. I'd never seen anything like it in person before, but I'd read about eyes like those. In romance novels.

"Thank you," I replied as coolly as I could. But I wasn't sure if my voice was working properly, and it's possible that I said "fruit moose" instead. Oh my god, why was I acting like a befuddled thirteen-year-old? I hoped I hadn't just said that last part out loud. I took my phone from him and stuffed it in the back pocket of my jeans.

"Would you like another cappuccino? You could take mine." He was holding another paper cup out to me. At this point, I could no longer look him in the eye. It's like I was... scared? Oh my gosh, that was it. I was now scared. I heard his voice say the words, and all I could do was pretend to look for my keys. Which didn't take long because I didn't have a purse or anything and they were just dangling from the front pocket of my jeans.

"Um, no thanks, I'm good. But thanks." I managed another quick glance at his face. His eyes were laughing. Were they laughing at me? Or with me? Well, I wasn't laughing. That meant he couldn't be laughing with me. So yes, he was probably laughing at me. Because here I was, a full-grown woman, acting like a big giant dork. On display, expressly for Mr. Cute Boots' amusement.

"Okay then." He turned to the counter to continue talking to Seth. I headed for the door as quickly as I could.

I stopped at the back of the shop and picked up a few extra napkins, because this episode didn't bode well for me driving with a hot beverage in the car, even if it was only half-full at this point. As I pulled a few napkins out of the dispenser, I heard Seth and the stranger laughing. I looked back at them, and he had turned back toward me. He was watching me, his eyes laughing a sparkly, silent laugh. Oh, sweet baby James, now they were both watching me. I wondered if there was any way I could salvage any of my dignity. I sighed disappointedly to myself. Probably not. I took a deep breath, flipped my brown shoulder-length curls, and sauntered out the door with what I hoped was a walk that looked good from behind. Because why the hell not.

SEVEN

THE DRIVE out to Al Turner's place was quite pleasant, and I was right—it was greatly enhanced by the enjoyment of half of a cappuccino. A whole one would have been nicer, but dorks couldn't be choosers. Al's place wasn't too far outside of town, but it was far enough out that the landscape changed over from old buildings and small neighborhoods to rolling fields and groves of short, scrubby trees.

Every time I drove around rural Oklahoma, it surprised me how much of the sky you could see. Especially compared to Manhattan, where the sky was usually just small pieces of blue, gray, or brownish-black that were visible between skyscrapers. But out here the sky was big, the ground was flat, and a woman could get to feeling a little lonely. But it was a good kind of lonely—the kind where you maybe felt disconnected from other people but very connected to the world around you. I sighed contentedly as I sipped my coffee. Some melancholy music would have completed the vibe, but today I had opted for silence.

As I watched the scenery go by, I had plenty of time to

contemplate what had happened in Hoboken. Why did I act that way? What made me turn into a tongue-tied klutz? I never did that in New York, not even in stressful business meetings and never ever over a guy. I must have gotten pretty good at keeping my defenses up in New York—both at work and at play. It was hard to admit to myself. But, to be fair, being tough was necessary sometimes. Maybe now I was softening up a bit, living out here on the prairie. Awwwww, how sweet. *Blech!* If "softening up" meant acting like an idiot in front of good-looking men, then I wasn't sure I wanted any part of it. I resolved to toughen back up.

My mind wandered to the fine piece of human engineering that had laughed me out of the coffee shop. Those eyes. I swear, they could cause traffic jams. Or worse. Political stalemates, union strikes, tsunamis. I wondered how many other women had spilled coffee on his boots. Or had died trying. Damn. It had been a while since I'd been inspired to think these kinds of thoughts about a man. It wasn't entirely unpleasant, even if he did cause me to turn into a bona fide oaf. But those eyes... My brain kept running itself in circles as I drove.

Google Maps informed me that in one thousand feet I needed to turn right, off the main highway and onto a smaller county road, so I slowed down to take the turn at a reasonable speed. Houses were set back from the road and situated on large pieces of land; the occasional fence delineated property lines and kept livestock from wandering. After a few more minutes, the houses became even farther spread apart.

All the deep thoughts I'd been having about making an idiot of myself in public plus a slight caffeine buzz had allowed me to forget I was about to interview someone who had claimed to see a mythical beast with big feet. But as I finally pulled into Al Turner's drive, I couldn't forget any longer. I turned off the engine and tipped the Hoboken cup to my lips one last time. Damnit. Empty. There was nothing left for me to do but get out of the car and face my fate. As I passed a gate leading to the backyard, I noticed a large fenced-in chicken coop along the side of the house. I heard a few soft, contented clucks and began to feel a little better. Chickens made everything better.

Time to get this fictional exposé started. I squared my shoulders, set my jaw, opened the screen door, and slammed the brass door knocker against its plate. I snorted as I came up with a "nice knockers" line to use in my book. No one answered. I knocked again—still nothing. I let the screen door close again and was about to turn and leave when the front door creaked open. Al then opened the screen door and poked his head outside to get a better look at me. His eyes were so squinty they were almost closed; it was as if this was his first exposure to sunlight today. His stubbled chin jutted out a bit, and his skin was so pale I began to wonder if he might be a vampire. I made a mental note to search online for *Guthrie vampires* as well as *Guthrie Bigfoot* as part of the research phase for the article.

Al silently waved me in, and after an extremely brief greeting, which consisted of me reminding him of my name and him grunting in acknowledgment, he turned and walked down a hallway toward his kitchen. As he walked, he held up his right hand and waved it around. I shrugged and made the assumption that this had been an invitation for me to follow.

"So you have chickens, huh?" I asked the back of his head. Silence. I didn't let it discourage me. "I just got some a couple months ago. Aren't they great?" More silence. It seemed my small-talk tactic wasn't working. I let it go, and we continued to walk down the hall in silence.

"Damn noisy things, always trying to get out," the back of Al's head finally griped as it and the rest of his body entered the kitchen. And here I thought everyone loved chickens. This was the second indication that something must have been wrong with him. The first indication was that he had claimed to see Bigfoot. Two strikes.

He sat down at a small table in the corner of the room. He looked like he might fall asleep sitting up. His eyes were still squinty, and he let out a big yawn. He picked up a nearby mug and started taking big gulps of whatever liquid was in it. Coffee? Bourbon? Both?

He motioned for me to sit and then started smoothing out the wrinkles in the blue-and-white-check tablecloth. A pile of bills lay in the center of the table, and a few opened beer cans were next to the pile. You could tell a lot about a man by what was on his kitchen table.

I sat down in the only other chair and pretended to rummage through my bag looking for my notebook and pencil. I knew I was just stalling because I really didn't know what I should ask him other than my one question I'd come up with earlier.

Finally I pulled out my writing gear and my phone and turned on its recording app.

"So you're new to the paper, eh?" he asked, cocking his head to one side to get a better look at me through what must have been his good eye.

"Yes, that's right. I've been there about three months now," I answered politely.

"I used to work at the *Ledger*. Did your fancy-pants editor ever tell you that?"

"No, he didn't," I noted, pretending to write something down. I could feel a doodle coming on. A good one, too.

"Yup, I used to work up on the second floor, as a layout editor." He took a few more gulps from his mug, a little flush entering his cheeks. I wondered again what was in the mug and if I could have some, too. It might make this train wreck go faster. Or at least take away some of the pain.

"Oh really," I said flatly. Out of curiosity I thought I'd ask Mark about this when I got back, but I had a feeling I was about to hear all about it right now. Ordinarily I'd love a distraction from having to talk about Bigfoot, but today I really just wanted to get out of that place, and I was going to have to think fast before this small detour became a major rerouting. "Oh yes, right," I recalled quickly. "I think I remember hearing about that now. Mark asked me not to talk about it, though. It's all confidential. Legal considerations and all that."

Al didn't say anything to this, but he had a confused look on his face, which I suspected wasn't going anywhere anytime soon unless I tried for another subject change.

"So. About your alleged Bigfoot sighting on Sunday," I continued. "Where were you when you supposedly saw the fictional creature?"

"Oh, now you know as well as I do that Bigfoot isn't fictional—he's real!" Al exclaimed, having just woken up. He sat up a little taller but lowered his head to look at me as if he were trying to peer over a pair of reading glasses. However, there were no glasses anywhere on his head.

I pretended not to hear this last remark. "So this allegedly happened sometime on Saturday? Or was it Sunday?" My pen was in hand, poised over my notebook, ready to write down the next words out of his mouth. Whatever they were.

"It was Saturday night. Well, maybe technically Sunday morning." He scratched his temple. "Or was it Friday? No, pretty sure it was Saturday. I mean Sunday."

I wrote a big question mark in my notebook. It was definitely time to start doodling.

"Me and Bill—that's Bill Turner, my cousin Bill—we'd gone over to Cedar Valley to visit our other cousin Frank. Frank Turner." He tried to take a look at my notebook, as if trying to make sure I knew how to spell TURNER.

So far, I was managing to keep up. *Al. Bill. Frank. Turner*.

"You saw this thing over in Cedar Valley, then?" I asked. I continued writing. *Cedar Valley*.

"Nope." He got up from the table and poured himself a glass of water from a pitcher by the sink. He set the glass back down on the table next to his mug, and I suddenly realized I was thirsty. "After me and Bill left Frank's place, I took Bill back to his house. In my truck. That one out there." He nodded his head toward the kitchen window, at an old Ford Ranger truck parked alongside the house. I made a mental note to not give a shit about the truck but finally decided to write *drove in truck* in my notebook just for a way to look busy.

"As I was driving to Bill's, that's when we saw him."

"Bill saw it, too?"

"Oh yeah, for sure he did. In fact, Bill saw him first. It was him what yelled out, 'Hey look, there's Bigfoot!'"

"How do you know it was a him?" I regretted asking it as soon as the words left my mouth.

"Well now." Al's face brightened considerably. Oh no. What had I just done? "That's a very good question!" he continued, "I was reading just the other day about the physical differences between male and female Sasquatches, based on some charts from the most recent data..."

I couldn't help myself. "So you saw this thing, in the dark, clearly enough to determine that its physical characteristics fell into the acceptable range of your questionable data enough to be considered a male specimen?"

"Huh?" Al's jaw dropped open slightly, and he squinted at me.

"How exactly could you tell it was male?" I tried again.

"Oh, that's easy. The lady Bigfoots always stay hidden. They're shy, you know." Al leaned back in his chair with an air of professorial knowledge regarding the gender characteristics of Sasquatches.

"All right, sure. So anyway..." I may have come across as a little too snippy, but goshdarnit, this was getting to be too much. I had to do something right quick, before he started showing me Bigfoot charts. Then I realized I was too late.

Al had turned around in his seat and pulled a stack of papers off the counter behind him. "In fact," he began, "if we review the most recent statistics, I'd say that based on the height of the subject and the width of the shoulders, we was definitely looking at a male specimen." He licked his bony index finger and peeled off the top three pages of the messy stack, but then thought better of it and shoved the entire pile at me. He pointed at a graph on the top page, trying to read it upside down. It didn't appear that he was going to continue talking to me unless I pretended to look at it, so I reached for my phone and snapped a photo of the entire piece of paper and shuffled through the rest of the stack, pretending to be interested.

"Oh, hmmm, I see, yes," I said slowly as I looked at a few more sheets. He looked pleased. I set the papers down on the table and assumed we were clear to continue. "Okay, so anyway, you allegedly saw the thing at your cousin Bill's place?" I asked.

Al scratched the side of his head, making the short, white, wiry hair stand straight out. It made him look even more off balance than I knew he already was. "Well..." He looked off in the distance, toward the refrigerator, which, as if right on cue, began to make a really horrible noise. I wondered if he had a Bigfoot in there. He still hadn't continued talking. I took a deep breath and started to count backward from a thousand. "Like I said, really it was Bill what saw Bigfoot first. We came to a sharp turn in the road, right before you get to the house." He made a curvy wave through the air with his left hand. "We were driving pretty fast, don't you know, and the headlights caught a big brown blob over in the tree line. Bill says, 'There's Bigfoot!' and sure as God's got sandals, there he was!"

I drew an X across the entire page of my notebook and put my pen down gingerly on the table before I lost control and stabbed Al in the eye with it. I figured I may as well ask a few more questions, though, to fill in my fictional account for the paper.

"So he was brown? How long was his hair?" I asked.

"Yep, this one was a rich chocolatey brown. They can range from brown to gray, depending on the time of year," he said with an air of someone who was very confident about their Bigfoot facts. "Same with length of hair. It's longer in the winter. 'Cause they get cold, don't you know."

Oh, this was too much fun. I was getting such good stuff for my novel—I mean newspaper article. "Al," I said politely, smiling my best friendly Oklahoma native smile at him, "you weren't by any chance drinking that night, were you?"

"Ah, well, there *may* have been a few beers involved. I'd had a few, for sure. Not as many as Bill, though. Also, I didn't have my glasses on. But none of that don't make no difference —I saw him! But when I drove back to Bill's later Sunday morning, I looked and looked and couldn't find any trace. But I tell you what, we saw that big hairy beast Saturday night all right!" He waved his hands in the air, getting more and more animated.

"Okay," I said, trying to placate him. "Sure, sure. And you didn't have your glasses with you, while you were driving home, in the dark, after having a few beers?"

"Nope. I forgot 'em at Bill's place when I picked him up earlier that night. Happens more than I'd care to admit, but don't worry. I drive without those damn things all the time."

"Uh-huh. Well, I feel better already," I said under my breath. "And why did you drive back to Bill's the next morning?"

"To get my glasses, of course. I can't see for crap without these glasses." Al started to push his imaginary glasses farther up his nose before he realized they weren't there. He looked around the kitchen helplessly. I knew I should help Al look for his glasses, but I really wanted to make it home before the weekend, so I pretended not to notice. I decided then and there that if I ever saw Al Turner's truck out on the road, I would call the sheriff's department immediately and take cover in the nearest ditch.

"Well, that's great, Al. Thanks so much for your time," I said, closing my notebook and getting up from the table. "I think I have everything I need here."

"D'you want to take my picture or anything? For the paper?" Al got up, too, and tried to straighten his wrinkled pearl-snap shirt.

"I'll let you know. If we need a photo, we'll send someone out from the paper. A photographer." I began to walk back down the hall toward the front door. "Thanks again."

"Sure thing, missy," said Al, who stayed in the kitchen.

As I walked down the hall, I happened to spy Al's glasses on the floor, just inside his living room. I picked them up and placed them on the small console table by the front door, and let myself out. I walked outside into the fresh, uncrazy air, got back in my car, and drove to The Book Store.

EIGHT

I GOT BACK to the bookstore from Al's place and reopened just in time for a massive crowd of one mom and three kids to come in. I love kids—as long as they're someone else's. I always figured that there was a very good reason that universal forces had skipped me over when it came to the maternal instinct and kept me out of the gene pool. I never questioned the fact that it just hadn't been in the cards for me. I mean, who was I to question universal forces?

I really did love kids—when I could watch them from afar. As far as children in my bookstore went, the jury was still out. It would always go one of two ways: either the kids would tear up the store and no one would buy anything, or alternatively, they would tear up the store and the parents would buy something so at least I'd get compensated for having to spend an hour putting the picture books section back together.

Today I was lucky enough to experience the latter scenario. Theresa Highsmith brought in her two daughters and one of their friends to pick out a few chapter books. I had met Theresa the month before, when she brought Bree and Becca in for Saturday Storytime, and we got to talking about romance novels. Books bring people together! Sometimes I wished we could just start a big ol' Book Club of the World and throw politics out the window, instead choosing to bond over shared stories. Maybe someday. It would be episode two of *Subversive Optimism*.

Having three energetic youngsters running around the store was a great distraction from thinking about my impending article assignment. I considered inviting them to stay longer and maybe ordering a pizza to be delivered so that I could procrastinate even more, but yes, I realized this was pushing it. And it would also be kind of weird. So when my customers were ready to leave, I let them.

I sat down behind the counter and took out my reporter's notebook. I was shocked—*shocked!*—to discover that there still wasn't much in there that I could use. I listened to the recording I made of my interview with Al. Not much there, either. Damn, this was going to be tricky. Even if I hadn't already decided to approach the whole thing as fiction, it was definitely going to take a few "artistic liberties" to make this work. Normally I wouldn't take any such liberties with a journalism piece, but desperate times called for desperate measures.

But before I could think of anything brilliant, I would need nourishment. I was really hungry. My mind wandered to sandwiches and then to that great deli on Fifth Avenue in Manhattan, their specialty sandwich minus the onions. I wondered if they were still open? Maybe I should google it. Did Mr. Cute Boots like sandwiches? If he was against mayo, this thing would never work. What exactly was I wanting to work? Ugh, work.

I thoroughly lost myself in my thoughts. As in, I couldn't find my way out of them. I had missed that left turn at Albuquerque, and I couldn't find my way back onto the freeway of normal thought. I was starting to think I might be lost forever, when the door to my shop opened and my dad walked in.

"Hi hi, Sweetie Pie," Dad said brightly. It was how he had been greeting me for as long as I could remember. The sight of him in my store and the childhood greeting acted like a switch, turning on the driver-assist software of my consciousness, and I was instantly jerked back into my lane. It gave me whiplash, but I was no longer out of control and careening down the Great Rumble Strip of Life.

"Hi, Popster," I said in response. He hated it when I called him Popster. I couldn't resist. "Where's the Monster? I mean Momster?" This wasn't the first time I'd made that Freudian slip and probably wouldn't be the last.

"She's parking the car," he said distractedly, not even noticing my error. He walked over to the front display table and looked over the titles. Or at least I think that's what he was doing. He squinted his eyes and leaned in so close to the new Michael Connelly novel that I thought he might try to lick it. Maybe that was why my mom was driving today.

Before I could say anything else, the door opened again and in came my mom. "Beverley, you really should clean those front windows. They're filthy!"

"Hi to you, too, Mom," I responded, trying to sound cheery. What on earth were they doing here?

"We were just driving through on our way home from Okarche," she chirped, as if she had read my mind. She absently ran a finger across my front counter to check for dust. We all knew that Guthrie wasn't anywhere on the route from Okarche back to OKC, but we all chose to ignore this fact. "You know how your father is about that diner with the fried chicken," she added as a disapproving aside.

"Still the best, Dad?" I asked.

"Still the best," he answered, patting his belly. A quiet burp emerged from his mouth, and he smiled. My mom smacked him on the arm as she passed him, and I tried not to laugh.

"Well, too bad you've eaten, or I'd invite you over to Stacy's Place for a sandwich," I said regretfully. I was secretly relieved. I just wasn't in the mood, what with Bigfoot and all.

"Oh, that's okay, dear. We're positively *stuffed*," Mom said. "But we'd love to see how you've come along with your house. Isn't it time to close up the shop?" She tried looking around for the nonexistent clock.

They had just crashed my house a few weeks ago. I didn't know if she was expecting me to have completely remodeled since then, or what she thought I was trying to do to a place I was renting, but clearly she thought it still needed improving.

"I'd love to visit with you guys, but I have a really big story I'm working on for the paper right now. I'm afraid it's going to eat up all my spare time for the next few weeks," I said earnestly.

My mom stopped milling around the front of the store and came to stand in front of me, one hand on her hip, the other crossed in front of her waist. "Honestly, Beverley," she scolded. "I don't know why you keep yourself so busy. How do you find time to get anything done at home? How will you ever find time to *date*?"

There it was. It had taken her approximately three minutes to press one of my buttons. I took a deep breath and tried to count to five. I made it to two.

"Look, Mom, I appreciate your concern. But I am fine. I

have plenty of time; I love both my jobs and everything just the way it is. I don't want to date anyone right now. I am perfectly fine by myself." I could feel my pulse quickening.

She shook her head and made those "tsk" sounds we all loathe to hear, especially when they're directed at us. "Well, you're not getting any younger," she pointed out. "You really should think this through, you know? You're running out of *time*, Beverly."

When I was little, my mom would tell me that I acted before thinking things through all the way. She would tell me this on a regular basis. Like, a million times a day. She had probably been telling me this since the day I was born, which was three weeks earlier than everyone had been planning for. I'm sure she held me responsible for that, too.

I'd been hearing this particular admonition for basically ever, but it really started bothering me when I hit those wonderful teenage years. Because when you're sixteen, you know everything, your parents are idiots, and everything they say is just *wrong* and who are they to tell you anything about yourself, anyway, what do they know? And then, the last thing you want to happen is for a kernel of truth to come out of the mouth of your mother. I started doing things without thinking them through on purpose. Nothing major, like I didn't burn down a grocery store or join the Young Republicans or anything like that. But if it was harmless and I knew it would bug my mom, I would do it.

My rebellious streak continued past my teenage years, as did my propensity to act quickly. When I was about thirty, I was finally willing to acknowledge that maybe my mom could be kind of right. A little bit. Sometimes. Possibly. It occurred to me around that age that this simple observation —acting without thinking things through—could explain a lot about where I was in my life and what was happening in it.

But making quick, intuitive decisions had come in handy in the publishing industry. I'd found a lot of great authors, and made a lot of money, by using this approach. But it also explained why I had a lot of never-worn clothes in my closet, a few (very large) regrets in the romance department, and a tenuous relationship with my mother.

Now in my forties, I was starting to learn. I'm not saying I never made quick decisions anymore, but I was able to think things through faster, and I definitely knew what I wanted in life more now than when I was younger. I was able to trust my intuition more, too. I was a late bloomer, but at least I was blooming. And I wished my mom would just give me a freaking break already. Sometimes she made me so mad that I wanted to stab the back of my hand with a... a... a stabby thingy. But no. Because with my newfound wisdom, I was wise enough to know what the right thing to do was.

I sighed and walked over to stand next to my mother, putting my arm around her shoulder. "Mom," I said softly, "I'm okay, really. Everything is fine, and everything is just the way I want it to be. Now, would you like to join me for a tea at the coffeehouse before you head home?"

She frowned at me, but it only lasted a few seconds. Her gaze softened, and she spoke softly like I had. "No thanks, dear, I think we're fine. I should probably just get your father home. He forgot his glasses and has been running into things all afternoon."

As if on cue, we heard a loud crash from the back of the store that sounded a lot like a ton of books hitting the floor.

"Sorry!" his voice trailed up from somewhere in the store.

"It's okay, Dad," I called back.

"Dear, it's time for us to leave. Beverley has lots of work to do," my mom yelled into the store. She gave me one last worried look, and I shot one back that said *really, I'm fine. Trust me.* We both smiled.

My dad wandered back to the front of the store, and we were standing in front of the door when we heard another giant crash. This one came from the roof.

"It wasn't me!" Dad said loudly as he threw up his hands in innocence.

Mom smacked his arm again. "Oh, don't be silly, Steve. We know it wasn't you." She turned to face me. "Beverley, you really should complain about the noise to your landlord. How can you have a nice quiet place for people to read with all this banging around in here?"

"Don't worry, Mom. That's just some guys fixing the roof. They'll be done soon."

"Your roof needs fixing? What kind of dump is this?" She just couldn't let it go. "I hope you've asked for a reduction on your rent."

"I've got it covered, Mom, really. Don't worry about it."

"Okay then, but honestly, Bev, you shouldn't take any shit from anyone."

My eyebrows raised in surprise. I couldn't think of what to say to that, so I just shrugged. Suddenly I pictured Mom and Leona going at it over rent reduction and repair negotiations. I made a mental note to call my mom in as my representative, the next time I needed something from Leona.

We said our goodbyes, and they left. That went reasonably well, I thought to myself. Maybe there was hope.

After a few minutes, the roof guys came in and assured me all was well up top, and I thanked them and reminded them to send the bill to Leona. I felt totally in control of everything. But it didn't last long. Bigfoot.

I still had a few hours before closing time. Back to focusing on my Sasquatch Problem.

For about three minutes, I considered simply quitting the paper. A great short-term plan, but a crappy long-term one. If the topic of Bigfoot was that important to this town, I'd defi-nitely be doing myself a disservice by quitting and refusing to take it on. Nope, I was stuck with it. I intended to spend the rest of the afternoon starting the article, but instead I drew a whole lot of little blob shapes on three pages of my reporter's notebook before finally calling it quits and heading home.

NINE

THAT NIGHT, I tried again. I sat down in front of my computer with my notebook, but the "BIGFOOT.DOCX" file remained blank except for my name and today's date. I did manage to take up some time by looking online for what I will call "supporting facts," but they were just really cheesy websites made by Sasquatch crackpots. I did discover a few interesting—or maybe just entertaining—things, however.

For example, it turned out that the legend of a "large, simian-like creature" was prevalent throughout American folklore. Most alleged sightings had been in the Pacific Northwest, and the word *Sasquatch* was actually a derivative of the word *Sásq'ets*, from the Halkomelem language of British Columbia. I wanted to find out what the hell Halkomelem was, but I decided to leave that for another day and get back on the Bigfoot track. My procrastination did have (a few) limits.

Another useful tidbit: while most Bigfoot sightings were in the Pacific Northwest, there had in fact been multiple sightings reported in Oklahoma. Which at least backed up the fantastical stories of a few loopy Guthrie residents. I also discovered the "Honobia Bigfoot Festival and Conference," held each fall in Honobia, Oklahoma, down in the southeastern part of the state. I found myself taking solace in the fact that Mark hadn't sent me down there to cover that hayride—yet.

I poked around the Honobia Bigfoot Organization's website, checking out this year's guest speakers which included two "doctors," a film footage expert, and someone who became obsessed after experiencing his own Bigfoot encounter. I was intrigued by the opportunity for *"campling"* at the festival site, thinking this might be some sort of fancy Bigfoot yurt-type experience. I was beyond disappointed when I learned that the promised *"campling"* offer was simply a typo and I was only welcome to plain old camping. Meh.

The Honobia Bigfoot Organization even had a scholarship program, raising money for local high school students to attend college. I could see it clearly—the summa cum laude of OSU thanking Bigfoot during her valedictorian speech.

My mind wandered further, and I tried to picture the people that attended the Honobia Bigfoot Festival and Conference. In my mind's eye, I saw lots of flannel. And beer bellies. And beer.

Most rational people thought that Sasquatch was a hoax. But it seemed that there was quite a large number of wackos —I mean, fine upstanding citizens—out there who took this stuff this very, very seriously. I wondered if they were all as drunk and nearsighted as Al Turner, or if they just had some sort of mental deficiency that left them devoid of all reason and logic. And weren't they afraid of this monstery beast? Surely I couldn't be the only one. But it seemed as if everyone else in the world was honoring Bigfoot, or looking for one, or writing erotica about one. It seemed I was in the minority—at least in Guthrie. If everyone knew I was afraid of them, it might be one more way I was stuck in outsider limbo. I started to feel like I was in a *Twilight Zone* episode.

I thought again about Al and his stack of papers that were his "supporting evidence." I was in a real bind. My Sasquatch star witness had been driving drunk, without his glasses, and saw a big brown blob at a turn in the road. Let's face it—that big brown blob could have been anything. It could have been a deer. Or a big piece of meatloaf. Or maybe Al's retina detached while he was driving. More than likely, it had been just a shadow. Or even nothing at all. I felt like I should relay this new information to Mark, in the hopes that he would tell me that on second thought, I should just skip the whole stupid thing. I had a feeling that in reality, he wasn't going to give a damn and would tell me to write it anyway, but none-theless, I felt compelled to try.

I still hadn't gotten anything written, but in an attempt to further the project, I decided to make one phone call. But to whom? Leona Tisdale? Bill Turner? The sheriff? I finally decided on Mark. I wasn't looking forward to it, but I dreaded calling him less than anyone else on my list. Plus there was that teeny tiny chance he'd still tell me to call it off. I walked around the living room a few times, seeing if I could come up with something to say besides "please don't make me!"

There was some saying about eating a frog that came to mind. It must have been left over from those days when I was really into that (short-lived) phase of productivity and creating good habits and setting goals and junk like that. If I were truly eating the frog, I'd just start writing the damn article already. Maybe tonight I was only eating the frog legs.

Which reminded me, it was getting late and I still hadn't done anything about making any dinner yet.

If there was any occasion that warranted an Emergency Beer, it was this one. I pulled one out of the fridge and dialed Mark's number before I could talk myself out of it.

"Ellison." I was pretty sure his cell phone had shown him who was calling and that he just answered the phone this way every single time to save time and emotion and avoid any extraneous verbal interactions. Or friendliness. I pictured him answering this same way when his grandma would call, or his proctologist.

"Hi, Mark. It's Bev," I said brightly.

Nothing but silence on the other end.

"Beverley Green," I added, knowing damn well he already knew which Beverley was calling him.

"Uh-huh."

I was reminded again of how much had changed since we were in eighth grade. Oh, how jaded some of us get. "Yeah, so, hi. Um, how are you?" I continued hesitantly.

"Busy."

"Okay, well, sorry to disturb you... so yeah... um, I think we need to trash the Bigfoot idea, see—"

"No. Just write it."

"Yeah, but our main witness—"

"Not trashing it."

"Well then, I'm going to need some more time to get it—"

"Nope. Sunday night."

His voice was smooth and sultry, a bit rough, and a little smoky. I wondered what in the world I could have caught him doing that made him sound like that. But sadly, that sexy voice just wasn't saying any words that I was wanting to hear. I tried one more time. "Okay, but Al Turner was—"

"Sunday."

Mark wasn't even going to give me a chance to tell him that Al had seen a giant piece of meatloaf while driving drunk without his glasses. And just like that, I knew there was no effing chance I could get a reprieve, let alone an extension. I wasn't even going to get a chance to try my last-ditch effort of giving him a fake excuse. Which was just as well, since I hadn't actually come up with one. Well, it had been worth a try. On to the next item of business. I was going to have to break down and ask about the expert.

"Okay, so in that case, like, where can I find Danny Cadence? Someone said you were friends with him."

"Danny? Why do you want to talk to Danny?" Mark sounded genuinely curious now, and I was thankful that he'd finally used a sentence that had more than three words in it.

"I, uh, I heard he knows a lot about Bigfoot," I said. I could hear Mark trying to cover the phone before he started laughing. He didn't quite make it. At least he was lightening up a bit, even if it was at my expense. "Look," I admitted, "I'm getting desperate here."

"Okay, okay," said Mark, his tone slightly softer. "I'll tell him you're looking for him, and I'll get back to you." He hung up without another word.

"'Kay, thanks, bye!" I yelled at the darkened screen of my phone. That big jerk! I muttered some choice curse words under my breath and took a big giant swig of my Emergency Beer.

TEN

WEDNESDAY MORNING FOUND me at the bookstore early again. I'd been waking up early the last few days, fretting about my assignment and having early morning nightmares of Bigfoot making me clip his toenails. Things really hadn't been going well this week, and I was hoping to at least catch a glimpse of the UPS guy as a sort of conciliatory prize. Granted, he wasn't half as intriguing or sparkly as the mystery man from Hoboken, but I was in the kind of mood where I would take what I could get.

The UPS guy may not have been my favorite person ever, but that was okay because I definitely wasn't his favorite person, either. Mostly because I kept admonishing him for leaving boxes on my doorstep while I was out. (I once had an idea to use this as a plot for a romance novel: *Spanking the UPS Man*, I would call it, and the tag line would be something like "he kept leaving his package in all the wrong places, and she wanted to punish him for it." I had written it down on my notepad but had never gotten back to it.)

At ten o'clock sharp, I opened my doors to let in all my

adoring fans. Which this morning consisted of the mail carrier with some bills, and a very nice gentleman who was looking for a copy of "Roger's Thesis." After a few rounds of verbal wrangling and some vague hand gesturing, I handed him a copy of *Roget's Thesaurus* and accepted his payment, and both of us were happy.

I was still waiting to hear back from Mark with information about his Bigfoot expert friend. As I waited, I worked on my marketing plan for The Book Store. I wasn't particularly fond of spending much time online (unlike those infernal Young People who went everywhere with their eyes glued to their phones), but I wasn't a total technophobe, either (like those people who, once they turned fifty-five, threw their hands up in the air, exclaimed "I can't keep up with all this shit!" and contracted a bad case of technological amnesia, suddenly forgetting how to use the TV remote). I was, as I always had been, quintessentially GenX. Caught in between the Baby Boomers and the Millennials, and ignored by marketers, financial planners, and health insurance companies, I and my fellow Xers flew under the radar most of the time. Truth be told, I was happy to be flying under the radar. My biggest beef with being GenX was that no one made a decent pair of reasonably priced pants for fortysomething women. But the positive aspects of being ignored by politicians, pharmaceutical companies, and cell phone manufacturers were infinite.

I had the unique ability as a "woman of my particular age" to bridge the gap between traditional media and publishing, and newer forms of marketing and promotion. So when I sat down to brainstorm ways to increase business at my bookstore, I had a lot of tools at my disposal. I just had to figure out which ones would work best in Guthrie. Guthrie was definitely a combination of new tech meets old school, and I wasn't exactly sure how to proceed. So I took out yet another notebook and started writing down all kinds of ideas. After a few hours of alternating between doodling in my reporter's notebook (procrastination), brainstorming, and shuffling books around the store (also procrastination), I decided that all that brain usage made me hungry and I deserved a midweek lunch at Stacy's.

I didn't snag my regular Monday booth, but I did get one in the back, where it was quiet and I could just sit and read while I enjoyed my lunch. I made myself comfortable and pulled out my Kindle Paperwhite. I was in the middle of a book that was surprisingly not a romance or even a chick lit novel. It was a crime fiction novel—*Faceless Killers* by Henning Mankell. A little Nordic noir was a great counterpoint to romance novels, and it was always fun to read books that took place in a foreign landscape. There was nothing like icy weather, only four hours of daylight during the winter, and a bunch of dead bodies to really make you appreciate the flowery happy ending of the typical romance novel. Plus I kind of had a thing for those noir heroes. You know—the strong, silent type with the hard exterior shell and soft, vulnerable underbelly who solved mysteries in their intense, quiet way. They had flaws, sometimes big ones, but who doesn't? Those flaws cost them dearly on occasion, but the noir hero always managed to do the right thing in the end. Because they had integrity and a defined jawline.

I changed up my usual order today, and instead of getting my beloved chicken salad sandwich, I went with a salad and a BALT minus the B. I wasn't sure "vegetarian" was a word used very often in a restaurant like Stacy's, so when I wanted a healthier alternative, I had to find work-arounds that everyone could understand. I wasn't vegetarian (obviously), but sometimes I liked to feel cool and progressive and extra healthy, so I would often go meat-free.

After I ordered, I settled in and continued to read my book, stopping only long enough to thank Bonnie for my food when she brought it and to take a giant bite of my sandwich.

I was so engrossed in my Nordic noir that I didn't pay enough attention to my sandwich-eating strategy, and the next time I bit into it, a big glob of avocado smooshed out from between the slices of bread, made a brief stop on my lower lip, and then landed squarely on the screen of my Paperwhite. It was a major eating fail, and an absolutely gigantic eating-in-public fail. When I looked around to see if anyone had witnessed said fail, I saw Mr. Cute Boots walking in the front door of the restaurant. I knew full well that "Mr. Cute Boots" was a really stupid name, but it was the first thing that had popped into my mind, so I went with it for now and made plans to admonish myself later. I quickly tried to duck my head, hoping he wouldn't see me, but alas, it was too late. Our eyes met—his had that radiant blue sparkle in them, and I suspected mine had that deer-in-headlights quality. And I was pretty sure I still had a blob of avocado on my face. I was also pretty sure he'd just smiled at me, but I couldn't be positive because I quickly lowered my head and searched for my napkin, which seemed to have disappeared into thin air.

I still maintained a faint hope that he hadn't recognized me and that I would find my napkin and be able to eat the rest of my lunch in peace. I used my finger to try to wipe the avocado off my face, and as I raised my head, I came face-to-waist with Mr. Cute Boots' shiny silver belt buckle. He had snuck up on me and was standing right beside my table. It was a nice belt buckle, and I somehow felt better knowing he strongly believed in secure pants. I looked up sheepishly, hoping against all odds that there was no more avocado on my face.

He looked just as windblown as before, and as if on cue, he reached his hand up and ran it through his curly hair like he was trying to smooth it out. My insides felt wobbly. It could have been from lack of protein, but I doubted it. That bastard. He was working it. I knew it, and he knew that I knew it, and he was obviously okay with that. He carelessly tossed his head back, his curls looking just as messy as before. It was his trademark move, I reckoned, and he knew it was my weakness. And the look in his eyes told me he knew it had elicited the intended reaction. That *bastard*.

As if all that wasn't bad enough, his blue eyes were sparkling at me. For crying out loud, whose eyes actually sparkled in real life? I'd been reading schlocky lines like that in books for years, but before I had met him, I had never realized that it was an actual thing. And that it would make me wobbly. I could feel myself blushing again, and that made me mad. What was next? Were my nether regions going to start tingling? Great googly moogly. If that was going to happen, the least they could do would be to have the decency to wait until I got home. I really hoped to hell I didn't still have avocado on my face. I wished he would just leave before the tingling set in.

But he had laughed at me the day before, in Hoboken. I didn't know for sure he was laughing at me, but it sure seemed like he was. That big jerk! And now he was here getting a close-up view of my avocado catastrophe. Not cool, Mr. Cute Boots, not cool.

Neither of us said anything for what seemed like forever,

so I finally figured I may as well get it over with. "Can I help you?" I asked in an annoyed tone. I kept looking around for a napkin and coming up empty-handed. It was as if there were no more napkins left anywhere in the state.

"No," he answered. He magically held out a napkin. I looked up at him, and the sparkle in his eyes had spread to include an equally sparkly smile. How did he always manage to have napkins for me? Did he carry around spares?

I grabbed the napkin and tried to wipe my mouth as casually as possible. "Well then, would you mind?" I asked, trying to look around his wonderfully proportioned body toward the door. "You're blocking my light." I smiled at him like I had a stomachache.

"You can just turn up the backlight on that thing," he said, pointing down to my Paperwhite. "Although, I think they work better without food on them." He tried not to widen his grin as he lowered his perfectly-shaped index finger to point at the blob of avocado that was still on the screen. In case I missed the fact that it was there.

The nicer he was, the madder I got. "Well, you're blocking my view, then," I snapped. I brushed his hand aside and picked up my Kindle. I held it over my plate and turned it upside down so that the avocado blob plopped onto the plate. I waved my napkin at him, and another blob of avocado fell out of it, back onto my Paperwhite. As it fell, I realized that I had just lost my last chance of coming out of this with any semblance of coolness. I made a mental note to search for a good psychologist later that afternoon, because I was going to need some help recovering from this lunch. I kept wishing he would just leave, but he kept standing there, looking down at me. And I was once again out of clean napkins. I started to get panicky. What did he want? Why was he still here?

Could we get a do-over where I didn't order anything with avocado in it? What was I supposed to do next?

Just then, a cell phone rang. It was close by. Wait. Now my left butt cheek was vibrating. My eyes went wide, but after a split second of being very disturbed by my vibrating butt, I realized it was just my phone in my back pocket. Saved! "Excuse me," I drawled as coolly as I could. I leaned to my right to pull my phone out of my left back pocket. "Hello?" I answered without looking at the caller ID.

He smiled at me and gave me a quick nod of his curly, sparkly head before turning and walking back toward the door. As I listened to a spammy mechanical voice telling me about my nonexistent overdue student loans, I watched him walk away. Damnit if he didn't look good from that angle, too. He probably looked good from every angle.

I hung up on the spam call and hung my head. I couldn't figure out exactly what had just happened. This was the second time that this guy had flustered me—whoever he was. I vowed that if we ever met again, if I ever had another chance and he didn't run away in the opposite direction first, I would keep my cool.

After my weird, messy, embarrassing, and confusing lunch (which was also delicious), I went back to the bookstore and looked for more ways to put off writing that damned Bigfoot article. I needed to talk to a few more people, and one of them needed to be this so-called expert. I tried to picture what this guy looked like. Earlier that morning, I had seen some pictures of the founders of the Honobia Bigfoot Festival and Conference when I poked around on their website. They were, uh, how can I put this nicely... they were not my type. And I imagined this Danny Cadence weirdo fitting in quite nicely with those nerds. I mean Sasquatch enthusiasts. Oh well, who was I to judge. Just because I didn't find guys who were into Bigfoot attractive, didn't mean they weren't catches for someone else out there. Just not me. So I pictured Mr. Cadence being about seventy years old, wearing thick glasses (when he remembered to wear them), sporting a big beer belly about to burst out of a plaid flannel shirt, with a trucker's cap that said I BELIEVE perched atop his slightly oversized head. Maybe he was also bowlegged. And wore a puffy vest. All the time. Even in the summer. I decided to send a follow-up text to Mark to see if he'd made any progress in contacting his buddy. Mostly because I just wanted to see what he looked like at this point.

Me: *Hey, have you by any chance gotten hold of Danny yet? For my article?*

Mark: *He hasn't called you yet?*

Me: *Was he supposed to? Does he have my number?*

Mark: *No text?*

Me: *Are we gonna just keep asking each other questions?*

Aaaaaaaaand I didn't hear back again. I knew better than to make Mark any angrier than he probably already was, so I gave up on finding the expert for now and decided to take another tack.

I checked my phone to make sure I had Leona Tisdale's contact information. I had hoped that maybe it had somehow disappeared off my phone but her number was still there. But maybe I'd continue to pretend it wasn't, just for a little while longer. Then I looked up the number for the Logan County Sheriff's Department and started to call them. I had to hang up again and do another search until I found the sheriff's name so I wouldn't sound like a total idiot when I called. Because I didn't know our sheriff's name. So sue me. Do you know *your* sheriff's name? It turned out he wasn't in, so I left a message for him, asking him to call Beverley Green with the *Ledger* as soon as he got a chance.

The rest of the afternoon passed quickly, even though I didn't hear from Mark, this Danny guy, or the sheriff. Once I got home, I spent some quality time with the chickens. They had been behaving themselves nicely for the last few days, although not really giving me very many eggs. I fed and watered them, and I asked again politely for some breakfast ingredients as I secured their pen for the night. I remained hopeful that I would be enjoying a delicious cheese-and-spinach omelet the next morning.

After a quick dinner, I decided that 6:49 was still early enough to call Bill Turner and Leona to schedule interviews for the next day. In this part of the country, "Prime Time TV" started an hour earlier than everywhere else in the United States. This was because out here on the prairie, we spent all the daylight hours tilling the soil and milking the cows. Then when the sun went down, we sat around by the light of our single kerosene lamp darning socks and reading from the Good Book. All activity stopped at 8:00 p.m. including watching sitcoms. So if I hurried, I could catch Bill and/or Leona before they started watching the final episode for the evening of Lawrence Welk on PBS, or whatever it was that the good citizens of Guthrie watched these days to get their kicks.

I dialed Bill Turner's number.

"Turner," someone said gruffly into the phone.

"Bill? Hi, this is Beverley Green, with the *Guthrie Ledger*."

"I think you have the wrong number."

"Is this Bill Turner?" I was a little confused.

"Nope."

I started to put it together—a little quicker than Al Turner was putting it together. "Al? Is this Al Turner?"

"Yes, this is Al." He sounded confused as to how I knew who he was.

"Al, it's Beverley. We talked yesterday about Bigfoot, remember? Hey, is Bill there? Can you put him on the phone please?" It shouldn't be this hard to call someone's house and get them on the phone.

"Oh, right!" Al said brightly, the light bulb finally coming on. "Yeah, hi there, missy. Sorry, forgot I wasn't at home tonight! Just a minute now." The phone bonked loudly on a hard surface, probably a countertop of some sort and hopefully not someone's head. I heard Al calling his cousin to the phone. I was so not surprised that these were the people who claimed they saw Bigfoot.

Bill came on the line, and after some mental and verbal finagling, I arranged to meet him the next day for a quick interview. He suggested meeting at Hoboken for coffee at noon. I was surprised yet very pleased by his choice of venue. It was a date.

Next, I took a deep breath and called Leona. I always got a little nervous when I talked to Leona. We'd had a few run-ins that I would not exactly characterize as friendly. Maybe they qualified as civil, but I always got the feeling that she thought I was up to no good. All the time. With everything.

"Hello?" she said innocently enough. Nonetheless, when she spoke, the tiny little icicles that made up her voice pierced my ears with cold.

"Hi, Leona, this is Beverley Green. How are you?"

"I'm fine, dear, thank you." That politeness. It was all a ruse, I was sure of it. "How are you?"

"Great, thank you for asking. Listen—"

"Did the roof get looked at on Monday? I got the bill—one hundred and fifty dollars, just for them to fix the roof! At least they *said* they fixed the roof. Did you see them working?" She just kept talking.

"It had a leak, and yes, they fixed it. They told me the roof was good as new now and would hold up fine through the winter." I hoped I was convincing her that the one-fifty she spent fixing the roof was money well spent, a bargain, and a small sum compared to what it potentially could have been.

"Well, I don't know," she said suspiciously. "Never had a roof leak before you moved in."

Quick subject change, before I got sucked in to a vacuum. "Look, Leona, I'm working on an article for the paper, and I was wondering if I could talk to you about your Bigfoot sighting last Friday? It's a very important article, so of course we wanted to talk to you." Flattery couldn't hurt, right?

"Oh really! Okay, sure, what do you want to know?"

"Could we meet somewhere tomorrow?" I was waiting for the other shoe to drop. Surely she was holding one above my head.

"Well, I'm pretty busy tomorrow. I have a hair appointment. So, no."

Thud. The shoe. Right on my head.

"Okay, no problem. Can I ask you a few questions right now?"

"Yes, but could you make it quick? *The Bachelor* is starting in a few minutes."

I inhaled slowly. "Of course, Leona, thank you. Could

you tell me what time it was when you allegedly saw whatever it was that was going through your trash?"

"Sweetie, I didn't *allegedly* see Bigfoot. There's a few of those beasts what live around these parts. It's common knowledge to those of us from around here." Ouch. I could feel my blood pressure rising.

"Um, okay, right. So what time did you see Bigfoot?"

"It was about 7:30 Friday morning. He knows that the trash gets picked up around eight, so he always comes before then, on Fridays."

I wrote this down. "It's interesting that he knows what day of the week it is," I observed, more thinking aloud than anything else.

"Well," she snapped, "he can probably tell from the position of the sun."

This made no sense, but it wasn't worth pointing out. I wondered if they also migrated with the seasons, or shed their winter coats in the spring, or maybe hibernated for the winter. I wrote a quick note to this effect so I could research it later. Or ask my Bigfoot expert. I knew I was going to regret asking Leona this next question, but I had to do it. "How do you know it was a male Bigfoot?"

"Because," she replied curtly in very matter-of-fact tone, "the females stay hidden with the babies. The males go out for food. Everyone knows this."

I wrote a little more in my notebook. *Traditional family values (Republican?)*

I realized I was going to need to do a lot more research. I wanted to ask Leona if she didn't think that maybe there were feminist Bigfeet (Bigfoots? What was the correct plural? Ugh, even more research) who made their menfolk stay home with the kids while *they* went out

94

and brought home the bacon. But I knew she couldn't really stand me as it was, and she happened to be in charge of how much rent I had to pay at the shop, so I skipped it.

"Do you have any proof that it, I mean they, I mean, um, he, raided your trash can?" I asked.

"As a matter of fact, I do," she answered quickly. "I had thrown out some expired Hostess Cupcakes. They were still in the box, and they were at the top of the trash pile. Then when I went out to move the can to the curb, I dumped in some more trash, some kitchen scraps y'see, and the box of cupcakes was gone! They love cupcakes," she confided knowingly.

Hardly conclusive in my mind, but then again, I was sane. "How about any footprints or anything like that?" I asked.

"Oh. Well, I didn't think to look at the *ground*," she said in a mocking tone, like I was an idiot.

"One last question for you." I added as much honey to my voice as I could muster for this old bat.

"Yes, what *is* it? *The Bachelor* is on now!"

"Would you know of anyone else I could talk to who might be able to give me some more information?"

"Try little Danny Cadence," she said without hesitation. "Oh hey, dear, *The Bachelor* just went to commercial, so there's one other thing I want to talk to you about now." My heart skipped a beat. I was half-curious, half-scared.

"Okay." I prepared myself for... well, I didn't know what, but I tried to prepare.

"I've been meaning to ask you. You're not raising chickens in your backyard, are you? Because a little birdie told me you might have some chickens. And chickens aren't allowed in neighborhoods in Guthrie. And certainly not in the backyards of my rental houses."

My brain tried to wrap itself around what it just heard. Leona was my landlady at home as well as at the shop? Oh, sweet coconut cream pie, this was just great. I realized I'd been silent a little too long and tried to think of something to say. Fast.

"Well," I laughed indignantly, "I don't know where this little birdie is getting their information, but I can assure you that I have no chickens anywhere except my freezer."

"Okay then, dear, I just had to ask. Because I'd hate for the property management company to come by sometime and find any chickens in the backyard."

"Yes, me too," I assured her. "Chickens—blech!"

"All right," she said sweetly and then hung up on me.

I immediately went to the kitchen and pulled out another Emergency Beer from the fridge. Apparently it had been a bad week because I was just about out of Emergency Beer, and it usually took about a month for that to happen. I sat down to process what I'd just heard.

First off, someone else had just confirmed that this Danny Cadence guy was a Bigfoot expert. He seemed to have quite a reputation, this mystery man. It seemed as if with each passing minute he was becoming ever more larger than life. I was excited to meet him, but also a little scared. However, he was proving to be as elusive to me as Bigfoot was. I just hoped he was better-looking. Or at least not as hairy.

Secondly, Leona was my dadbern landlady twice over? Whaaaat? This was almost too much to process. This was what happened when you went through a property management company—you didn't always know who actually owned the house you lived in. Now I was finding out that Leona was my landlady for two separate properties. And this was about two places too many. Guthrie was proving to be quite small. And I didn't know who the "little birdie" was that spilled the beans about my illegal chicken operation, but I suspected he drank a lot of beer, had trouble finding his glasses, wasn't actually all that small, and chirped way too much to his friends. I was confused, though, because my neighbors Zach and Zoe had chickens. I wondered if they knew their brood was illegal? Thinking back to the many times I'd smelled pot smoke coming from their back porch (not that I would know what that smelled like; I was just guessing, mind you), I figured that even if they knew chickens were illegal, they probably didn't give a flip. I wondered if I should have a chat with them to see what they thought. I made a note to research the neighborhood covenant and the city and county rules for animal husbandry. I supposed I needed to come up with some kind of action plan now, some kind of chicken contingency plan. Because I, too, would hate it if I got busted by Leona for having chickens.

ELEVEN

I GOT up early Thursday morning and went on a quick run. By "quick" I mean "short" and definitely not "fast." I used to go to the gym regularly when I lived in New York but hadn't really kept up with it in Guthrie. I just hadn't had time. And I figured that between walking to work, walking almost everywhere else, and lugging books around all day, I was getting a pretty decent workout. But some regular cardio is always good, and we all have to start (back) somewhere, right? Thirty minutes walking/jogging through my neighborhood seemed like great progress. Plus it was getting to be a nice time of year to be outside.

I took a shower, scrambled a few store-bought eggs (still nothing from my hens), and wolfed them down with toast, fruit, and coffee. I walked to the bookstore and again admired what a nice day it was turning out to be. A little less humid, a tiny bit cooler. We were still a while away from the leaves turning, but signs of fall were starting to appear.

It was a little over a mile to the shop, and I got there just in time to open the front door for business at ten. No one but me was there, but still. I got down to business nonetheless.

I spent the morning doing some light accounting (sales were actually pretty good overall!), and figuring out my best-selling genres (crime fiction, yes! Politics, not so much!). I was pleased at the amount of success I was having so far running an independent bookstore in a small town. Of course sales could always be better, but I was doing okay. What with online bookselling pretty much taking over the universe, running a physical bookstore was kind of like trying to run a Popsicle stand in Iceland in the dead of winter. Tough, but not impossible if you knew how to market your Popsicles.

After puttering around the store a bit more and making a few sales, I once again returned to my reporter's notebook. Time to get to work on the article; I couldn't put it off any longer. I looked over my notes and then turned to a blank page. I looked it over, too. Then I put the reporter's notebook aside and reached for my novel notepad. Time to work on something else. I decided to doodle some hexagons today.

Around 11:30 I closed up the shop and put my fancy "GONE TO LUNCH" sign on the door. When I had first opened the store, Kelly gave me the coolest gift—a set of signs to hang on the front door. There was "OPEN," "CLOSED," "GONE TO LUNCH," and my favorite (but not often used) "BUSY WRITING - COME BACK LATER." Each one was screen-printed on a yellowed page from a large old dictionary and then laminated for protection. I smiled every time I used one. She was so good at giving gifts, unlike me. I was more of a gift-card giver. You buy whatever you want and just think kindly of me when you got whatever it was, and we could call it good.

I walked over to Hoboken, found a table, and pulled my

lunch out of my bag. Seth didn't mind if I ate in the shop sometimes, as long as I bought coffee and left a big tip. As per our arrangement, he made a cappuccino without me ordering one, and when it was done he walked over, put it down in front of me, and picked up the cash that was waiting for him on the corner of the table.

I continued to wait for Bill, pulling out my Kindle and picking up where I'd left off in the Mankell book. It was a dark read, and after a few pages, I started to feel like there was a gloomy gray raincloud hovering over my table. I got the urge to read something a little more... sunny. I took a break to look around the room, and my gaze landed on Grace from the *Ledger*. She'd come for coffee on her lunch break. Or rather, she had come for two coffees on her lunch break. There was an iced latte on the table in front of her and a second one across from her, placed in front of an empty chair. It appeared that she had invited her "boyfriend" out for coffee—so cute. I hoped that one day the perfect man would suddenly materialize in that empty chair across from her, pick up the coffee, take a drink, and propose marriage. Oooh! Could this be an idea for a romance novel? I got out my notebook and started scribbling.

I didn't have time to write much before Bill came into the shop. He called out my name and waved at me and then got in line to place an order. As I waited for him, I cleared my lunch off the table to make some room and made sure my reporter's notebook was open to a fresh, doodle-free page. A few minutes later, he made his way to the table holding a small, fancy wooden plank. There were two drinks on the plank: a cortado and a small glass of sparkling water. My eyebrows raised in surprise; I had pegged him as more of a Folgers kind of guy and figured he just came to Hoboken for the pastries or the cute hipster girls.

"Hi there, little lady!" he said brightly, putting his complicated drink setup on the table. You could tell that Bill and Al were related—they both had the same messy, white hair and round jawline. But while Al was wiry and lean, his cousin Bill was shorter and a little rounder. And had a much more interesting T-shirt collection, it seemed. Today's featured a screen-printed photo of Madonna, circa 1985's *Desperately Seeking Susan* look. It was pulled tightly over a large round belly.

"Hiya, Bill, good to see you. Thanks for meeting with me today," I greeted him as he sat down across from me.

"Oh, anytime, missy! I love to talk about Bigfoot!" He drew his chair closer to the table, not bothering to lift it off the floor very much before doing so. The sound it made was exquisite.

"Hey, I didn't know you were such a coffee aficionado," I said, gesturing toward his drink setup. I wasn't above drawing out a conversation about coffee to avoid one about Bigfoot.

"Well," said Bill as he tried to lick the crema off his mustache, "I mean, what the hell's the point of bad coffee? I'll drink cheap beer all day long, but if I'm gonna have me a coffee, it needs to be good. None of that burnt, diabetic coma–inducing Starsitsplace coffee." He waved his hand dismissively toward the front door.

Something made me look in the direction he had waved, and there, standing right inside the door of the coffee shop, was Mr. Cute Boots. He was wearing faded jeans today and a dark blue T-shirt that fit just right; it hugged his torso in all the right places. He was practically glowing with cuteness. A veritable cute aura came off him, and I swore I heard angels singing. But actually, it was just Bill prattling on at me.

"You okay, hon?" Bill asked. I turned back to look at him, and his face was asking, "are you smart enough to follow this conversation, or am I going to have to slow things down for you?"

"Huh? Oh yeah, sorry, Bill. Yes, I agree. Good coffee is of the utmost importance," I said slowly. My gaze made its way back to that blond-haired muse as he walked to the counter to order. His gait was smooth and confident, and I became acutely aware that my inner monologue was sounding more and more like a romance novel as I watched him. He had spotted me and shot me a lopsided grin. His eyes sparkled again. My pulse quickened ever so slightly, just like you read about in those damned books. This was getting ridiculous! I started to wonder if he had some kind of superpower; it was as if my eyes just couldn't look anywhere else but in his direction. Snap out of it, woman! I yelled at myself inside my head. To no avail. Absolutely no part of me was listening. We were all mesmerized by the sparkles and the sinewy muscles. It was as if he got better-looking every time I saw him.

"Yup," said Bill. It appeared that he had inhaled his cortado, because the glass was empty and he was slurping his sparkling water as a chaser. "Third wave, all the way." He burped loudly and then laughed.

Oh, right. I was sitting at a table trying to interview a guy wearing a Madonna T-shirt about his Sasquatch encounter. My mind made its way back to the conversation at hand and became incredibly confused between the visual of Bill Turner with his crema mustache and his unkempt head of thinning white hair, and the words that had come out of his mouth about the subtleties of third wave coffee. This planet never ceased to amaze me. There were some truly astounding feats of nature out there. Like Bill, and bugs that look like plants, and that weird deep blue hole in the ocean floor off the coast of Belize.

"So," I began, "you and Al saw Bigfoot last weekend, huh?" I took a sip of my cappuccino and tried not to ogle that blond guy out of the corner of my eye. So far I hadn't been very successful.

"That's right. We was driving home in Al's truck, and the damn thing nearly crashed right into us!"

I started writing in my notebook. Never mind that his story already contradicted his cousin's earlier version. I thought I'd just hop on this spaceship and see what weird planet we ended up on.

"How did that happen?" I managed to sound interested.

"You know how you see those old safari movies where the giant Land Rover is driving through the African desert and a big ol' rhino rams right into the side of it? Well, it was like that. Only in Guthrie. And we were in a Ford."

Before I could open my mouth to ask Bill what the hell Bigfoot was doing ramming himself into the side of a Ford truck, that handsome stranger had sidled right up to our table, without me noticing. I just looked up, and there he was. I felt like I was in a Land Rover, on safari. Quick, where was the button to roll up the window, damnit? This rhino looked like it was ready to charge! I took another sip of my drink, hoping the casualness of the act would somehow cover up my fear. I was pretty sure rhinos could smell fear. Plus my hand was shaking like a leaf during a fracking earthquake—a dead give-away of my unsteady inner landscape.

"Hi, Bill," he said, smiling down at us. "How's your coffee?"

"Oh, just perfect, Danny, just perfect. I think Seth's got the grinder dialed in just right today."

I almost spit out my coffee. Was this *the* Danny? The man that'd been following me around town laughing at me was the guy I needed to talk to? Or was this just *a* Danny? It seemed too coincidental. Oh, this was just great.

He turned his gaze toward me. "You've got a little some-thing—" He reached down and almost touched my face, and I was about to die of fear like the tourist in the Land Rover on safari. But instead of making contact, he just handed me a napkin and pointed to the corner of his own mouth, to illus-trate. "—just there," he said.

I was freaking mortified. I was a well-functioning adult who was tidy, didn't smell bad, and knew how to eat and drink without smearing food all over herself. Yet every time I saw this guy, something seemed to go terribly, terribly wrong. I started to think maybe I was cursed. I made a mental note to search for "women in 40s cute guy curse" on the internet when I got back to the shop, to see if there was a cure. While I was thinking all this, I grabbed the napkin he was holding out to me and wiped my face down like I was drying my windshield at a car wash. Seriously, what was his deal with napkins?

"Thank you," I said as daintily as I could.

I noticed his hand was still extended, this time without a napkin in it.

"Hi," he said, extending his hand farther toward me. "Daniel Cadence. Nice to finally meet you." He smiled a sparkly smile.

I took a deep breath. I supposed I should attempt communication. I looked in his eyes just long enough to say that I had done it, but not too long that I would get sidetracked by their sparkliness, or even worse, completely derailed. I reached out my hand and took his, and we shook.

"I'm Beverley Green." I tried to sound calm and in control. I was just happy I had remembered my name. To my knowledge there was no longer any food on my face, nothing had dropped on the floor, and no piece of clothing was malfunctioning. I might be able to make it through this encounter. I watched our hands shake amicably. I watched as they got to know each other. My hand felt warm, protected, and not too overwhelmed. My hand approved. It wanted to go on a second date.

"You can call me Danny," he said slowly, also watching our hands shake. It finally occurred to me that he wanted his back. I let go.

I stood up. "Okay, great. Thanks, Danny." Maybe he had forgotten that I was rude to him the day before. Maybe he didn't recognize me from Stacy's or our previous meeting here in Hoboken. "So I understand that you're an expert on, um, Bigfoot." I said casually.

"Well, yeah, I guess so. I mean, I've seen a few over the years, and I seem to have acquired a fair bit of knowledge on them." He looked down at Bill, who was still sitting. Bill nodded emphatically.

Before I could figure out the answer to the question of whether or not I should invite him to sit down, he looked at me, shifted his weight from one foot to the other, and said, "Listen, I've really got to get going, but it was nice to officially meet you." He sparkled at me again, nodded to Bill, and turned to leave. The rhino had left the building.

Bill watched me watch Danny walk out the door. "Nice kid, that Danny," he said with real affection in his voice. "Now, where were we?" He slurped up the rest of his sparkling water. As I turned back to him, the look in his eyes told me that he knew exactly what I had been thinking about Danny Cadence. Bill was confusing me. Perhaps he wasn't as clueless as I had first thought. I did my damnedest not to take his bait.

"You were telling me how Bigfoot rammed into the side of your cousin's Ford like a rhino on safari," I said pointedly.

Bill burped again. Louder this time, and still with no thought of apology. "Oh yeah, right. Yep, the darn thing charged the truck!"

"Which side?"

"What?"

"Which side of the truck did Bigfoot charge, the driver side or the passenger side?" I wanted to see how far he would run with this.

"Well, my side of course. The passenger side. If you check Al's truck, you'll see, plain as day! There's some big ol' scratch marks on the door!" He raised his arms as if to show me how humongous the scratch marks were. I threw a look of impressed amazement onto my face for kicks.

"So Bigfoot needs a manicure?" I asked casually. I wrote this part down and then made a mental note—this could be the premise for an interesting romance novel. Albeit a super weird one. "What was she wearing?"

"I didn't say it was a girl Bigfoot," he countered.

"True. But you didn't say it was a boy Bigfoot, either. Whatever it was had long nails, right? So girls have longer nails that boys, right?" I knew all of this was hooey, but I really just wanted to see how long we could stay in this particular eddy. "Unless they're metrosexual," I added as an afterthought, opening up a whole new door leading to Bigfoot sexuality that upon further reflection, should probably stay shut for now.

"I guess." He looked down at the ground, not seeming to know what to say next.

"So? Was she wearing anything?"

Bill was clearly flustered by all this, but now a renewed resolve showed on his stubbly face. "She wasn't wearing anything," he said defiantly.

"Wow," I said. "So just to confirm, you saw a naked female Bigfoot filing its nails on your side of the truck?" I really wanted to ask him if he saw any Sasquatch boobs, but I didn't get a chance before he started talking again.

"Look here, missy," he said sternly, shaking a finger at me. "Is this an interview for the paper or an inquisition? I know what I saw, okay? I saw Bigfoot on Saturday night, and so did my cousin. The thing attacked our vehicle. I'm lucky to be alive today, to be here talking to you." He got up to leave. Apparently my own luck was running out and he'd reached his limit. "You're new around these parts, see? You don't know how things are or what our history is. You don't believe me? Well, that's your problem. Go check my cousin's truck. And then get your darn facts straight and write this up all proper, like it should be." He turned toward the door and headed out, his "as seen on TV" Velcro-closure man sandals shuffling loudly across the hipster reclaimed hardwood floor.

TWELVE

I LEFT Hoboken shortly after Bill did. As I walked back toward my shop, I took a few deep breaths. It felt good to be in the fresh air and sunshine, especially after being told off by a crazy person. I wondered if he had meant "cross-examination" instead of "inquisition." It was hard to tell for sure. It could have been a mistake, but I'd never been to court in Guthrie, so it was possible their legal system could be a bit more antiquated than I realized, resulting in unusual questioning procedures. At this point, nothing would surprise me about this place. I made a mental note to ask Kelly about the local legal inquisition system. It might make a great article series, once this Bigfoot stuff died down.

I didn't know whether to laugh or cry at having been told to "check my facts" while writing a Bigfoot sighting article. It definitely made me want to cry from having been accused, once again, of being an outsider. I wondered how long it would take me to become anything but, or if I ever would. I asked myself that question again. The one about why I moved here.

Even so, I just couldn't stop wondering if there really was a Lady Sasquatch showing off her hairy high beams all over town. I tried to get this visual out of my head, but it had been floating around in there since Bill adamantly declared the thing they had seen was a girl. Naked Sasquatch Lady. Definitely *not* an idea for a romance novel.

I took a little detour and went over to the Apothecary Garden on Oklahoma Avenue. Mrs. Karchner was there, pulling weeds by the lemongrass, and she gave me a little wave. I smiled and waved back, my faith in humanity somewhat restored. Maybe it was the friendly wave, or maybe it was the afternoon sun in that bright blue sky, but suddenly I felt a little more resolve and resolution. Suddenly I had a little more motivation, and I was more determined than ever to do whatever it took to make friends with those Guthrie residents who just weren't having any part of the Beverley Bandwagon yet. People like Leona, Al, and Bill. What was their problem, anyway? Just because they were old enough to remember how great things "used to be" didn't mean that things couldn't get better now. It's like they were a gang or something, a gang of old-timers. The Guthrie Old-Timers. Yeah. I wondered how many more there were, whose crazy I hadn't yet run into. I couldn't wait to find out. Anyway, I was going to befriend those damn GOTs, come hell or high water. Or alternatively, I wouldn't let them bother me anymore. I'd show them that it was all like water off a duck's back. I was the duck.

Just then a fat, noisy Canadian goose flew overhead and dropped a poop present on the sidewalk right in front of me. That was close! What was it with me and bird poop, I wondered. I sighed loudly. In some cultures, getting hit by bird poop was good luck. In which case, Monday's Chicken

Poopageddon had guaranteed me a very charmed life indeed.

I decided to look up some bird idioms later. Not because it would be a good way to procrastinate or anything, but because it might come in handy for my romance novel. You never knew.

I left the garden and continued my walk back to the shop, heading toward Division Street. My mind wandered and I continued to think of bird idioms (and then that turned into thinking about bird metaphors and then from there, chicken salad). I looked around to see where I was, and that was when I spied Al's truck parked in front of Craddick's Barber Shop, right across the street from where I was standing. I casually crossed the street, pretending to window-shop, but quickly realized this was bad cover since the storefronts on either side of the barbershop were empty. I just looked like I was loitering. Which I was.

I nonchalantly turned away from the buildings and toward the cars parked along the street, letting my eyes linger a few seconds on Al's old Ford Ranger. I hoped it didn't look like I was trying to steal a car. It was probably what people would assume, but I couldn't help that right now. I just didn't want them to think I had such bad taste in cars. I checked the passenger side of the truck and sure enough, there were three long scratches along the door and the front half of the side of the truck bed. The scratches were so deep, they had left bare metal exposed, so it was plausible that they were new because the metal hadn't rusted yet. Hmmm. I wondered why Al didn't mention the damage to me when I'd interviewed him on Tuesday. Maybe he hadn't noticed the fresh set of Shesquatch love scratches on his vehicle? Or maybe he'd been drinking before the interview and just forgot to mention them. Or they actually had nothing to do with a damn Bigfoot sighting. My logic revved its engine, peeled out, and did one big loud smoking donut on the asphalt of my brain, and I gave up. I started walking down the street before someone decided to call the sheriff's department on me for suspicious truck ogling.

I didn't get very far, though, before I heard someone call my name. I turned back around, and there was Al coming out of the barbershop, waving at me.

"Hiya, Bev!"

"Hi, Al. How's it, uh, going?" For some reason I had almost asked him how it was hanging but caught myself at the very last minute. It was information I just didn't need to know.

"Oh, pretty good, pretty good. Say, how is the Bigfoot article coming along? Do you need my picture?" He had caught up with me, and we stood in the street, our hair blowing in the strong Oklahoma breeze—mine across my face, his straight up off the top of his head.

"It's going well. I'm almost done," I lied. "And I will double-check to see if they want a picture of you," I lied again. They were tiny lies. I figured they were okay. "Oh hey, I do have another question for you, though," I added.

"Oh yeah?" His face brightened. "Okay!"

I nodded toward his truck, which was a few parking spaces down from where we stood. "I noticed you have a few big scratches on the side of your truck. How did you get them?"

"I do?" He looked at his truck. We could only see the driver's side, so he started walking toward his vehicle and went around to the passenger side. "Well, would you look at that!" he exclaimed. He seemed genuinely surprised to see them. I guess he didn't look at the passenger side of his truck much.

"How did they get there?" I asked.

He folded one arm across his chest and scratched at the stubble on his chin with his free hand. "Well now, I'm not really sure," he said slowly.

"No idea how long they've been there? Or anything?" I thought I'd give him every opportunity to give me an unprompted Bigfoot encounter story, but no such information seemed to be forthcoming.

"Hmmmm." He was still scratching at his stubble. "I guess it could have been my cousin Mildred."

How many cousins did this guy have? And were they all as crazy as he was? I knew I was going to regret asking, but there was no way I couldn't do it. "How did your cousin scratch up your truck?"

"Well, she got kind of mad at me the other day. And she does have sharp fingernails."

"Al, I seriously doubt a woman could scratch paint and primer off the side of your truck with her hands."

"Well, you don't know Mildred!" he replied quickly, his eyes widening with fear.

"True." He had me there, I had to admit. "Well, I sure am sorry your truck got all scratched up, in any case." I watched him for a moment, still standing there staring at the side of his vehicle. "Welp, I gotta get going. See you later, then." I waited a few beats for him to respond, but it seemed he was lost in thought. I turned on my heel and walked down the street toward my store. Whatevs.

I thought as I walked. He didn't say one word about a close encounter with a Bigfoot, like his cousin Bill had sworn to. I would think that the driver of the truck would remember the sights, sounds, and truck damage associated with being attacked at close range. Someone was exaggerating. Or lying. Or both.

Once I was back at the shop, I checked my phone and saw that I had a message. It was the property management company who was in charge of my house. Oh, great. I put the phone on speaker and pressed Play.

"Hello, Miss Green, this is Allan from Prairie Wind Property Management. We'd like to come by and visit your home on Saturday morning for a quick inspection, as requested by the property owner. Of course, we need your permission to enter the home, but we will be coming by at ten o'clock to speak with you. Thanks, and have a great day."

Oh cripes. If I declined, they'd think I had something to hide. Which of course I did. And if I said yes, they'd see the chickens, and Beryl would probably do something terrifying, like try to eat the poor guy. I considered my options for a few seconds and then decided to do what any sensible person would do in this situation. Forget about it.

Next I called Kelly to tell her that I finally had met Danny Cadence.

"Oh yeah?" she asked after I shared my news. "How did it go?" It sounded like a loaded question to me.

"What do you mean 'how did it go?'" I asked defensively, just in case I was right.

"I don't know... what did you think of him?"

"I guess he's okay," I said thoughtfully.

"Okay?" she repeated. "Just 'okay'? What does that even mean?"

"I don't know—what do *you* mean?"

"The man is a god among men, Bev. Or are you so smitten with your chickens that you didn't notice."

Oh, I noticed all right, but I thought it would be best to keep my enthusiasm to myself. He might inspire me to write a complete twelve-book romance series, but if I said anything more than "meh" to my friend, it might also inspire a whole lot of gossip or teasing. And I didn't need any of that right now.

"Meh," I said, with a shoulder shrug I was pretty sure she could hear over the phone. She sighed annoyingly. "It turns out I've run into him a few times before today, only I didn't know it was him," I continued, thinking back to the Phone Dropping Fiasco and the Great Avocado Splooch Incident.

"Well, it's a small town—you were bound to run into him at one point or another."

"Just as long as I don't literally run into him, we'll be fine." As I said this, I imagined three or four different scenarios involving "running into" Danny Cadence, which, upon quick reflection, didn't seem all that terrible.

"So how's the article coming?" She changed the subject. I could tell she thought all of this was hilarious. It pretty much was, I had to give her that.

"I haven't started it yet."

"Don't you have to turn it in on Sunday?"

"Well, there's nothing like waiting till the last minute to turn out the best-quality work." I was trying to convince both of us. "I've got plenty of time to get this thing done. If I could just..."

"You have no idea what you're doing, do you." She read my mind.

"Well, I have a general direction picked out. I just can't quite figure out the exact angle here." This was the truth. It felt like all I was getting was lies, or crazy stories from crazy people. Or both. I still couldn't even figure out which was which.

Kelly spent about five more minutes engaging in what I would call "laughmonishing"—admonishing me for not having started writing the article yet, and laughing at me for having to write it in the first place. When I couldn't take any more of it, I told her some customers had come into the store and I needed to go.

"Okay," she said. "Good luck with Danny."

"Yeah, okay, bye." I didn't really register what she had said until after I hung up. Good luck with Danny? Wha?

I allowed myself a few minutes to reflect upon the sparkly-ness that was Danny Cadence. At our last meeting back at Hoboken, I had managed to get a good look at his hands. They were strong hands, with long fingers and clean, perfectly shaped nails. They were the hands of a Greek god and they said "I have got everything under control here, so just don't worry about it." Just thinking about his hands made the sun shine brighter out in the street, and I swear I heard those damn angels singing again. Kelly was right. There was no denying it.

On a procrastinative whim, I changed out the display in the front windows of the shop. I took down the biography books and put up a romance display. I was feeling optimistic. Even with the new enticing display, no one came into the shop for the rest of the afternoon, and I ended up falling asleep at my desk, or taking what we procrastinators like to call a "power nap to refresh and renew the senses." Yeah, that sounded way better. During my power nap, I had a dream. About Sasquatch. I awoke from it in a cold sweat. The dream definitely would not have been a good plot for a romance novel.

THIRTEEN

Late in the afternoon I officially pronounced my workday over and done. It was late enough to count as a full day but still early enough that I had to try to justify closing up. Oh well. Thank goodness I was as good at rationalizing as I was at procrastinating.

I started walking home but somehow ended up standing in front of the *Ledger* offices. I may as well go in and see what was going on, I figured. It was the end of the day, and most likely no one was there. Most likely I was just procrastinating some more.

I entered the building, and it was quiet on the first floor, except for the faint sound of shuffling paper coming from Mark's office, which was located along the main hallway. I quietly snuck by and avoided detection. I meandered toward the back of the building and up the stairs to the second floor. No one was up there, so I walked slowly to the bay of windows at the front of the building, which looked out over West Cleveland Avenue. I looked at the shape of the windows and the moulding details along the ceiling. It was a beautiful old building. I had looked it up once; it was built in 1891 and had been home to Guthrie's newspaper since 1894. I thought about Al Turner working up here all those years ago, and what it must have been like back in his day. I wondered if Sasquatch had ever applied for a job as a copy editor.

As I looked down onto the street, I saw Danny walking toward the building. He walked right up and I lost sight of him, but he appeared to have entered the front door. Oh great. He probably came by to see Mark. I wondered why I hadn't ever seen him here before? I mentally mapped out different routes that would allow me to escape the building without being seen from Mark's desk. But unless I wanted to set off the emergency-exit alarm back in the break room, I was going to have to walk right past Mark and Danny. I considered it. But, as much as I would have loved to avoid Danny for fear of falling on my face—or worse—maybe I did need to talk to him about Bigfoot. I was going to have to eat the whole frog this time, and I was going to have to go talk to him. I took a deep breath and walked down the stairs, heading straight for Mark's office. They hadn't seen or heard me coming yet, and I could hear them talking.

"You never mentioned her before," I heard Danny's voice say.

"She's only been working here a couple of months," Mark replied quickly. "It just hadn't come up."

"Were you not wanting me to meet her?"

"Don't be ridiculous. I told you to talk to her for her upcoming article, didn't I?"

I wondered if they were talking about me. Who else could they have been talking about? Grace maybe? I hoped they were talking about me. I decided to give myself the benefit of the doubt and assume it was me.

"That's true," Danny sounded thoughtful. "But still."

"But still what?"

"Are you going to ask her out?"

"She's my employee, Danny."

"Cool."

"But I guess I've thought about it," Mark added, as if he didn't want Danny to think he was completely counting himself out of the running.

"She sure is something, isn't she," Danny pondered. What the hell did that mean?

"What the hell does that mean?" Mark asked him.

"It means the lady's got some zazz," Danny replied. His voice had so much pep, I could picture him making jazz hands as he said the word "zazz."

I silently asked myself a question, and once again, Mark asked it for me out loud. "What the hell is zazz?"

Danny laughed. "She makes me laugh," he answered. I wondered if this was just because I fell over, had stuff all over my face, and acted like a nervous schoolgirl around him.

"She's funny, smart, and a real knockout," he continued.

Oh. My. Goodness. Was I power-nap dreaming again, or was this for reals?

"For cryin' out loud, Danny, no one calls anyone a knockout anymore," Mark laughed at his friend.

"Well, I'm gonna call her a knockout, anyway," Danny stated defiantly.

"She looks just the same as she did in high school," Mark said, with a little hint of wistfulness in his voice. "And she is damn smart. A woman's got to have brains to be sexy, in my book."

"That's for damn sure," Danny concurred.

"But I don't care how much zazz she's got, she's still got to finish that damn Bigfoot article."

At this point, my rational brain reminded my fluttering heart that I hadn't actually heard either of them use my name, and that it was still entirely possible that they were talking about someone else. My fluttering heart said, no way! They are totally talking about me! And my rational brain retorted with yes, it is probable, but I need conclusive proof. The fluttering heart responded with, Don't be a dumbass! Mark mentioned the Bigfoot article—how many other women around here are cute *and* happen to be writing Bigfoot articles? My brain admitted that was a pretty valid point. I told both of them to shut the hell up, and in the hubbub, I forgot to be quiet and I let out a little cough. Gosh darnit to heck and back. Everything went silent in Mark's office.

I quickly started walking toward the office so it looked like I had just come downstairs and had not in fact been eavesdropping for the last few minutes. As I passed Mark's open door, I looked in innocently and followed that up with a fake double take. "Oh hi, guys!" I said brightly. I hoped I was being convincing.

"How's the story coming, Bev?" Mark asked me, his dark eyes hooded and guarded. Not even a "hello" to my face, just work. He was probably nicer to his garbage man than he was to me in person.

"Almost done," I lied through my teeth. It was a lie so big it actually made my teeth hurt getting it out. "I just need a few more... facts," I added, my eyes moving from Mark to Danny, who was sitting on the edge of Mark's desk, smiling at me.

"Anything I can help with?" Danny asked.

"Actually, yes," I said, trying to sound as brainy as possible. "Could I ask you a few questions about, you know, Sasquatch?"

"Sure!" He sounded very excited about this. "Right now?"

Mark stood up from behind his desk. "Well, it can't be here. I've got to close this place up and head out. The kids are coming over to my place tonight—I've got to get home and make dinner."

Danny looked sad. I had an idea. "Do you have time to walk me back to my shop? We could talk on the way," I suggested. I didn't actually have to go back to the shop, but it seemed like a good excuse. I mean idea.

"Perfect!" His face brightened.

I turned back to Mark and gave him a little wave. "See ya, boss. And remember to poke holes in the plastic wrapping before microwaving the Lean Cuisines." I turned on my heel and Danny followed me out of the office and back outside.

We started walking slowly back to my shop, which was just a few blocks away. I was ready to get down to the questions and pulled out my phone to start recording our conversation.

"So how are you liking Guthrie so far?" he asked me.

I knew that small talk was an integral part of regular, everyday human interaction, yet I had been so focused on the Sasquatch thing that his question took me by surprise.

"Oh." I raised my eyebrows as I thought about this. "Well, I guess I like it quite a bit, actually." I realized as the words came out of my mouth that they were really true. "How long have you been living here?" I asked him.

"I'm from here," he answered quickly. "I inherited some property from my dad, and his dad had left it to him. So, the

Cadence family has been here for a while." He slowed down his pace so that his longer legs would keep pace with my shorter ones.

"Wow," I said, thinking this through. "You must like it, then."

"Yep, I do. I actually do a fair bit of traveling, but I always love coming home again. I wouldn't want to live anywhere else."

I would have loved to continue learning more about him, but we were almost back to my shop and I really needed to talk business. I hit Record on my phone.

"So if you've been living here all your life, you've seen this alleged Bigfoot thing, then?"

"It's not alleged, Bev. Our local Bigfoot population is the real deal. And yes, I've seen a few of them over the years."

"Here?" I meant Earth, but he probably thought I meant Guthrie.

"Yes, within the county," he confirmed.

"How about lately?"

"I was out of town for a while, but I got back about a month ago, and I haven't seen any since I've been back. But there was a time, a few years ago, when I'd see them pretty regularly, on the road between my ranch and town." We were walking slowly down the sidewalk, and he turned to look behind us, as if making sure we weren't being trailed by a Bigfoot or two.

My mind was turning. Where did he go when he traveled? How long was he usually gone? He owned a ranch, not just a house? Did he have horses? Or chickens? What about a pool? Instead I simply asked, "On the road into town, is that where most of the sightings are?"

He laughed. "I have no idea where most of the sightings

are. I think a lot of folks see them around, but they don't bother calling the sheriff or doing anything about it. I can really only speak for myself. I live northwest of town; it's about a fifteen-minute drive to my place. I've seen them up that way on occasion."

I stopped walking, and a second later he stopped, too, and turned to face me. "You can't seriously believe in this stuff," I said softly.

"Oh, but of course I do," he said earnestly, matching the softness of my voice. A serious look came over his face. "Everyone around here does."

I shook my head incredulously and sighed. There was just no way! "Well," I said as I thought of what to do next, "is there anything you can tell me that might be relevant to this most recent sighting, or that might help me write a 'serious' article?" When I said the word "serious" I pulled my index and middle fingers down through the air and immediately hated myself for being that person that used air quotes.

"I can tell you all kinds of things," Danny replied. He turned, and we continued walking. "Usually you'll see males closer in toward town. The females tend to stay hidden. And they seem to have an uncanny way of figuring out when trash day is. They like to raid full garbage cans. You know, right before the trash truck comes."

Hmmm. This backed up Leona's story about her Bigfoot sighting. Did I now possibly have to kind of believe these people might be telling the truth? I turned my head and looked at him, and he had a big sparkly smile on his face. "Oh I see," I said angrily, "you're just messing with me. That's all a load of hooey about the trash cans and whatnot. Okay, seriously, can you tell me *anything* useful?"

"I'm not lying!" he said, full-on laughing now, his hands rising in surrender.

"Then why are you laughing at me?" I asked.

"Oh," he said between guffaws, "you should see your face. You look terrified!"

I wasn't sure that someone being terrified was all that hilarious, but we *were* talking about Bigfoot, so really I guess it was pretty hilarious. But still. Damnit.

"I so don't believe you. Nice try," I snapped at him.

"No, I'm really serious! You've done some research, right? Sightings have been recorded ever since the town was founded. The fascination with Bigfoot is part fact, and yes, okay, maybe a little part fiction. But only part. Everyone likes to embellish, but that doesn't mean we don't still take it seriously. And believe me, people will be reading your article with a critical eye, and they'll be double-checking your facts."

Well, this was just great. Before now, I was worried about how to make it a convincing article. Now I had to worry about being "fact-checked" by the whole damn town. Did anyone do this when I wrote about the fire department getting new boots? How could you even fact-check stuff on Bigfoot, anyway? I remembered Al's messy stack of papers full of facts and figures. Oh.

He could tell I was lost in thought. "Would it help if you actually saw one yourself?" he asked.

My eyes bugged out, and I stopped walking again. "Whaaaaaat?"

"Yeah, I could take you on a Bigfoot stakeout, if you want," he said. His eyes brightened even more, as if that were even possible. "Would that help your story at all?"

I briefly considered his offer, but then I came up with one

big, giant, emphatic *nope.*

"Thanks," I said politely, trying to think up a good excuse before I continued talking. After a few beats, I came up with one. "Sadly, I just don't think there's time for that. You see, I've kind of waited until the last minute to write this article." I was so relieved that I had come up with a great reason not to go on a monster hunt.

"I see," he said thoughtfully. "So it's not because you're scared of them or anything like that?"

"What makes you think I'm scared of them?"

"Most people who are new to town don't know much about the local stories, and, well, you seem pretty jumpy when you talk about Bigfoot."

"Pish!" I dismissed him with a wave. "I scoff at your local stories. I'm not scared, and I was born in Oklahoma, damnit. I just think it's all incredibly stupid."

"Really." He put a hand on his hip.

My defensiveness was turning into anger. He was kind of right, damn him. I wanted to yell at him that I wasn't scared. I wanted to stomp my foot and declare *I am a local!* And I wanted to go on that stakeout to prove my bravery. I did a darn good job surviving in New York by not showing any vulnerability, by proving I was tough.

Yeah, except I knew he was right. Part of me wanted to drop that toughness now. Maybe I didn't need it anymore. Maybe this time, I could try the truth instead of getting mad and defensive.

"Yeah, I mean, you know I'm just from OKC, right? It's forty-five minutes away, but I still think that counts as local. It's not like I'm from Tulsa or something. But you're right about me being scared of Bigfoot. I'm actually petrified. Have been since I was a little girl." I looked down at my feet. There. That wasn't so bad.

Danny laughed, and I could feel my defenses going back up. "I understand," he said with compassion in his voice. "Lots of people are scared at first. But Sasquatches really are harmless for the most part."

Maybe he did understand and wasn't making fun of me. We walked in silence for a while, and finally we were at the door of my shop. I wondered if he was being quiet because he was disappointed that I was scared of fake monsters. "This is my stop," I said. I stood at the door, expecting him to say goodbye and walk off so I could continue home.

"Can I come in?" Danny asked. "There's a book I've been looking for."

"Oh, sure," I said. I unlocked the door and walked in, holding the door open behind me so he could follow me in. Who was I to decline an opportunity for a sale? I closed the door behind us, and when I turned back around, Danny had disappeared down one of the narrow aisles. I wondered which book he was looking for. I sighed and walked behind the counter. I was going to have to start writing this infernal article pretty soon. At some point.

Just as I began thinking about new ways I might be able to continue procrastinating, Danny walked up to the counter with a book. It was *Faceless Killers* by Henning Mankell. The same book I was reading. Coincidence?

"It's okay to be scared of Sasquatch," he said. "I mean, those suckers are big, and scary-looking. They don't ever do much, though. They usually keep to themselves and only come out when they're good and hungry. They do love Hostess Cupcakes. But still." He placed some cash on the counter. "It's also all right that you're from Oklahoma City, it's all right that you lived in New York, and it's all right if some people don't think of you as a local. Sometimes, having outsider status can come in pretty handy."

He smiled at me, with those sparkles and those blue pools of liquid awesomeness. I was speechless. "Call me if you change your mind about the stakeout. I know some good places. We can go anytime." He turned and left the store. I swore his narrow hips taunted me as they sidled out the store.

I was still standing there, staring at the door through which he had just left. I was thinking about what he said. And then I was wondering how I could call him, since I still didn't have his number, and Mark didn't seem to be all that helpful. Oh well. I sighed and rang up the book. As I picked up the pile of money he left me, I noticed a scrap of paper amidst the bills. His number was written on it. I placed the money in the till and the scrap of paper in my pocket. I didn't want to lose it.

I gathered my things together and prepared to leave. Again. It was later now, and the sun was just going down. I had procrastinated so much that now I was going to have to walk home in the dark. Which wasn't the end of the world, but sometimes I worried that I wouldn't be seen by crazy Oklahoma drivers. Like Al Turner. And yeah, I supposed I should be concerned about my overall safety at night. However, I had survived New York, so I was pretty sure I could survive Guthrie.

I was heading toward the front of the store when I looked up and noticed a large figure was filling up the entranceway to my shop. In the murky light, I couldn't see anything but his large personage. At least, I assumed it was male. Did I mention it was large? And by large I mean tall and broad.

And because he was tall and broad and I couldn't see his face, he was also menacing. I had just been thinking about crazy people, and good lord, now it looked like one was on my doorstep. Oh my god, was it Bigfoot? Wait, did they wear cowboy hats? I was pretty sure I could see the outline of a cowboy hat on the monster's head.

I stopped in my tracks and tried to figure out what to do next. Could I hit him over the head with the latest Stephen King novel? Or at least bruise his shins with it? This was ridiculous. I was starting to think I saw Bigfeet everywhere. Were they really everywhere and I had simply managed to live in blissful ignorance up till now? I silently cursed Guthrie, and made a mental note to complain about the lack of disclosure in tourist literature at the next town meeting.

As I was debating my next move and wishing I had learned karate, the menacing figure opened the door to my shop and walked in.

"Are you Beverley Green?" Sasquatch asked me in a deep voice.

"Ummmm." I still wasn't sure what angle to take here. I casually placed my hand on the nearest Stephen King novel, conveniently located on my front display table, and quietly clawed at it.

"I heard you were looking for me."

My knees almost buckled. How on earth did Bigfoot hear I was looking for him? Were they clairvoyant? He sure did have a nice voice, though. But damn, those guys were way better connected than I thought. I wondered if they used cell phones or just their Bigfoot Collective Consciousness. "Ummmm..."

Sasquatch took off his hat and stepped farther into the store. My eyes were about to bug out of my head with fear. I readied the Stephen King novel. Wait. Now I could see that it was not a Bigfoot at all, but rather just a very tall man.

"I'm Sheriff Branch," he said, a slight smile showing at one end of his mouth. I must have looked petrified with fear.

"Oh."

"You had some questions for me? For an article for the paper?"

"Oh. Oh!" My flight-or-fight response began to stand down, and my brain started working again. "I'm sorry, Sheriff, you kind of scared me. I thought you were Bigfoot." I let go of the Stephen King tome and slouched in relief.

"Bigfoot?" he asked, raising an eyebrow.

"Long story," I said matter-of-factly. "Well, it's not a very long story, actually. But anyway. I was wondering if I could ask you a few questions about Bigfoot."

He raised the other eyebrow. "Okay," he said. "Shoot."

I found this word slightly disquieting coming out of the mouth of the Logan County Sheriff but thought I'd put my faith in the law and dispense with the small talk. He didn't look like the type to engage in it, anyway.

"Yes, okay, so." I reached for my bag that was sitting on the display table and pulled out my reporter's notebook. "Is it true that you had a few people call in Bigfoot sightings last weekend?"

"Yup," he answered.

"How many?"

He was silent.

"Is there, uh, any way you can tell me who called them in?"

"Nope."

"Was it Leona Tisdale and Al Turner?" I tried again.

He shrugged his shoulders. They went way up toward

his ears, then floated back down again, as relaxed as could be.

"How often does this sort of thing happen?" I asked, trying a different tack.

"Oh, every few months or so. Some people call them in regularly, others more sporadically. Just depends."

He started looking around my shop. I hoped he wasn't seeing anything illegal. It was a feeling I got every time I looked in my rearview mirror and saw a police car, or if I was standing in line with a law enforcement official at the grocery store. When I saw the police, I just automatically felt guilty for no reason at all. Busted, for selling books! Oh, policeman fantasies! Mental note for romance novel idea...

"It depends? What does it depend on?" I watched him take in my store.

"Lots of things," he answered. He started walking down an aisle, toward the mystery section. "Full moon, tax season, election cycles..." He disappeared out of view.

I put down my notebook and rubbed my temples. This guy was turning out to be even less help than Al and Bill Turner had been. I didn't even know what to ask next. Before I could think of anything, he reappeared with a book. He placed it on the counter. It was *The Man Who Smiled* by Henning Mankell. The fourth book in the Wallander series. The series of which both Danny and I were reading book one. This guy was three books ahead of us. My jaw dropped.

He pulled out his wallet. "How much?" he asked.

"On the house. Can we consider it a donation to local law enforcement?" I thought it would be a good gesture to be nice to the law.

He smiled his slight smile again and shook his head. He

dropped some money on the counter and picked up his book.

"Is that all you needed?" He looked at me as he turned toward the door.

"I, well, I'm not sure. I really was hoping you could provide me with a little more insight into this whole Sasquatch BS." I put his money in the cash box and prepared to leave again, gathering up my book bag and taking out my keys.

"I'm afraid I don't have much insight into that," he said slowly. "And I'm not entirely sure it's all BS."

"Oh." I wanted to ask him what he meant, but I had a feeling I wouldn't get an answer, even if I asked.

We walked out the door together, and I locked it behind us. He put his hat back on and snugged it down toward his ears.

"Well, thanks, Sheriff. Thanks for stopping by." I smiled and gave him a small wave before turning and heading for home.

"Where are you parked?" I heard him ask behind me.

I stopped and turned. "Oh, I walked to work today."

He took a step toward me. "Let me drive you home. It'll be safer. You never know."

I thought about turning him down but then decided maybe I shouldn't say no to a direct request from the sheriff. "Are you sure?" I asked.

He lowered his head at me so that his eyes were barely visible below the brim of his hat. Oh. Yes, he was serious. "Okay. Thank you."

We walked to his vehicle, a white Ford Explorer that said SHERIFF on both sides in big black menacing letters. I started to feel like I'd done something wrong again. He opened the passenger door for me, which was a good sign—at least he wasn't making me sit in the back like a prisoner. He got in behind the wheel and pulled out into traffic as I gave him directions to my house.

We drove a few minutes in silence, and then I couldn't stand it anymore. "Do you think this is an unsafe area?" I asked. I wondered why he had offered me a ride, and if maybe I should stop walking to work.

"Nope," he answered. There was a pause, and then he continued. "You just never know."

Well, I couldn't argue with that.

I decided to take another chance. "Do you yourself believe in Bigfoot?" I asked. It had become clear he wasn't going to engage me in any conversation, and since I couldn't stand the silence, I would have to be the one to remedy it. "Have you ever seen one?"

I watched him as he screwed up his face in thought before answering. "I don't think I've seen one myself, no. I mean, there's been a few unexplained and unexplainable things I've seen during my time here, things that could maybe be credited to the existence of Bigfoot, but I haven't actually seen one myself."

"Yes, but do you believe in its existence?" I needled.

"Well now, that's kind of a personal question, isn't it?" He looked at me, his expression completely unreadable.

We pulled up in my driveway, and he put the Explorer in park but left the engine running. My time was up.

"Okay, well, thanks again for the ride, Sheriff, and thank you for your help." I got out of the vehicle, and he tipped his hat to me.

"Let me know if you need anything else," he said pleasantly.

"I will," I assured him. Although I knew I wouldn't get

anything else out of him, even if I did need it.

I closed the big car door and watched as he backed out of the driveway and disappeared down the street. Well, that was a total bust, I thought to myself. It was too bad he didn't actually turn out to be Sasquatch—at least then I would have gotten more information for my article, even with the language barrier.

I walked in my house and threw my bag down on the living room floor. This was all just so wonderful.

FOURTEEN

I STARED FORLORNLY into the empty abyss that was the inside of my refrigerator for several minutes. It was an existential experience, and I often did it to decompress from stressful days. When I started to feel guilty about wasting so much energy by keeping the door open for so long, I headed out to the backyard to put the chickens to bed. As I went to unlatch the door into the pen, I noticed it was undone. Uh-oh. Something was definitely amiss. There were no chickens to be seen. I peeked inside the coop and discovered that the chickens had put themselves to bed and were all tucked in for the night. But something about the whole thing was too calm. Ah, right. Beryl was missing.

I did a quick head count, and everyone was there except for her. So she had somehow managed to unlatch the pen and make an escape. Either she hadn't invited anyone along, or this time none of the other birds thought it would be worth their time to head out for a nighttime romp.

How on earth had she done it? Either she was some sort

of freaky escape artist chicken, or there was some fowl play afoot. I would put money on the first option.

I latched the pen again and looked around the backyard—no sign of her. There was no telling how long she'd been out or how far she had gotten this time. "Beryl!" I hissed. Not that yelling her name would send her running home, but I was frustrated and it was all I could do. "Beryl! Damnit!" I said louder, looking around some more. I started walking to the side of the house.

"Hey." I heard a man's voice. It was my neighbor Zach. "What's up? Did you like, lose someone?"

"Yes!" I exclaimed. "A chicken. Have you seen one running loose anywhere?"

I kept walking toward their fence, and now I could hear some dub reggae playing. I could smell the ganja weed (again; not that I knew what that was or anything. But I had read about it on the internet. For research. In college).

"Um, no," said Zach. "But you could come check if you want. The gate's open."

I doubted that Beryl was so close to home, but I thought it was worth a try. Maybe they were so high over there that Beryl was right in front of them and they didn't know it.

"Okay." I left my yard and walked to theirs, opening the gate to my neighbors' backyard. He and his wife, Zoe, were sitting in the cool evening air, listening to music and partaking of the aforementioned recreational herbal substance.

"What's up?" Zoe raised a hand toward me—a hand that was offering me a little cigarette-looking thing.

I waved a hand at her, politely declining a hit. "Hi," I said. "I lost one of my chickens. Beryl. Big Catalana, crazy eyes. You haven't seen her, have you?" I looked around.

I had spoken to my neighbors in passing a few times, mostly about chickens. But we hadn't ever really had any meaningful conversations, and I hadn't ever been in their backyard before. They had a larger chicken pen and coop than I did, and a really nice vegetable garden. "Nice backyard!" I nodded with approval as I spoke.

"Thanks," said Zach. "We haven't seen any loose chickens around tonight, have we, babe?" He turned to Zoe and took the joint from her.

"Nope, sorry. It's been pretty quiet back here tonight," she said, exhaling a cloud of smoke. "We'll keep an eye out for you, though," she added helpfully.

"Thanks," I said.

Zach squinted at me. "You sure you don't want any?"

"Well, I'd really love to, but I need to get some work done tonight," I replied, which was true enough. "I'd appreciate it if you'd let me know if you see or hear Beryl," I said as I turned to leave, satisfied that my AWOL chicken was nowhere near the area.

"Will do," Zach whispered on an inhale.

"Oh hey," I said, thinking of one more thing, "can I ask you guys a quick question?" I turned around again.

"Sure," said Zach, letting out his breath.

"Do you guys by any chance believe in Bigfoot?" I was truly curious. I was a GenX woman, and I was cynical and pessimistic (or in other words, realistic). But Zach and Zoe were Millennials; maybe they were even more pessimistic than me when it came to blood-curdling beasts. Maybe they grew up learning to question everything.

Without missing a beat, Zach answered me. "Oh hell yeah." Zoe nodded silent agreement. Well, so much for my theory.

"Really? Have you ever, like, seen one?" I asked.

"Nope," answered Zach. "But I've heard lots of people around here talk about Bigfoot, and I met someone once who saw one. Just because I haven't seen one yet doesn't mean I don't still believe they exist." He bobbed his head to the music. It was more of an answer than I had gotten out of the sheriff in the thirty minutes we had spent together.

"I've seen one," Zoe said casually. Zach spun his head to look at her.

"No shit? You never told me that! For reals?"

"Yeah." She took another toke and held it in for a few beats before continuing. "About six months ago. Me and Amy were down by that pond at your dad's place. I guess I just forgot about it till now."

"No shit," he mumbled again as he kept looking at her as if he had a new-found awe for his wife.

"Are you sure?" I asked. Maybe I had a new person to interview for my story.

"Well, we had done mushrooms, but still, yeah, it was a Bigfoot for sure."

"Oh, cool," I said. Never mind. I turned to leave again. "Well, thanks. I was just wondering. Seems like he's a pretty popular mythical beast around here."

"Dude, he's not mythical, okay? Mythic maybe, but definitely not mythical." Zach sat up straighter. "He's the real deal!"

"Yeah, sure" was all I could think of to say. I wanted to debate the nuances between "mythic" and "mythical" with him, to understand what he meant exactly, but I was afraid it would take at least three hours and two bags of Doritos to get through it, so I decided against it. I didn't have the time, nor the Doritos. "Well, you guys have a good night, and thanks again." I took off for my house.

I looked at my quiet coop, and I thought about getting in my car and driving around to look for Beryl. But it was dark, it was late, and I had so many other things to do. Honestly, I was starting to believe that maybe it was for the best if Beryl disappeared. She would no longer be around to incite her cellmates to insubordination or violence. Of course I would miss her, and I hoped against all odds that she would be okay out there, but I decided that maybe I needed to let her go. I hung my head and said a silent prayer for her safe passage to wherever she was headed. Now it was time to face the music. Article writing. Right after some dinner.

I tried the wasteland of the refrigerator again and came up with enough healthy ingredients to qualify for a quick veggie stir-fry. After inhaling dinner and then thoroughly cleaning the kitchen, I decided that the living room needed dusting. As I dusted, I thought about Danny's offer to take me on a Bigfoot stakeout. I thought about the sheriff's answers that just left me with more questions, and about my neighbor's drug-induced Sasquatch sighting. None of it made any sense in my brain. My brain was about to go on strike.

I got another Emergency Beer out of the fridge (if not this week, then when?) and watched some really stupid TV show, something about baking pies with nothing but household cleaning supplies. Or something like that. I wasn't really paying attention. When it was over, I was no closer to knowing what to do and my deadline was looming closer and closer.

Holy cheese on crackers. This town. It sure felt like I was the only sane one in the state. Tonight, Guthrie was a big, lonely city full of crazy people. Wait. Maybe I was the only crazy one. Oh. It was all in how you decided to look at it. Regardless, it was still lonely.

I stared at my bookshelf, full of books not written by me. I just had to start writing this article. I just couldn't bring myself to do it. And I still had no idea where to begin exactly. But finally, after another Emergency Beer, I pulled out my laptop and my notebook and stared at both. I did manage to get a few paragraphs down and was deep in thought when my cell phone rang. I looked at the time before I answered— I'd been sitting there for an hour and a half.

"Hiya, Kelly," I sighed in place of a real greeting.

"That good, huh?" she said in place of a real greeting.

"Let's just say I'd rather be at the dentist's."

"Cleaning or filling?"

"Root canal."

"Have you started?"

"Yeah, I have an outline in progress," I sighed again.

"What angle are you taking?" I knew she was trying not to laugh. I just didn't care anymore. I was completely beyond trying to save any of my journalistic dignity.

"You'll just have to wait and see," I scolded. "I ran into Danny again," I added.

"Oh yeah? Not literally, I hope."

"Har-har. He kind of offered to take me on a, uh... Bigfoot stakeout."

This time she didn't try to hide her laughter. She let out a big old hearty guffaw. "You're not really thinking of going, are you?"

I was silent. She burst out laughing again.

My face screwed up in anger and frustration. "Look," I huffed. "I'm desperate here. I don't know what else to do. I need help with this thing. Never in a billion years did I think

I'd be facing *this* kind of writer's block." I had wanted to ask for her advice, but she was not being very supportive. But I probably would do the same thing if I were in her shoes. She didn't have to know that, though.

"This wouldn't have anything to do with the fact that Danny Cadence is extremely good-looking, would it?" she asked. This thought had crossed my mind, but I'd immediately dismissed it and focused on more rational, logical reasons why I would consider going, like facing my fears and writing a good article. Because I am one of the best rationalizers alive today. But damn her and her skills of perception.

"Oh please, like I'd be that transparent," I scoffed.

"Okay then," she said, in that tone people use when they don't believe a word you are saying.

"You really need to give me more credit than that, damnit."

"Sure, sure."

"But, um, actually, can I ask you a question?"

"Sure." She said the word quickly and sharply.

"So, like, um, is Danny, you know... single?" I was pretty sure I knew the answer to this question, but my rational brain wanted to double-check the facts.

"Why?" Kelly asked. "Is it relevant to your article?"

I exhaled loudly. "Noooooooo," I said. "Of course not. I'm just curious. I heard him and Mark talking, and... well, I was just wondering." Please just answer the damn question already, woman!

"Yeah, I'm pretty sure he's single right now. He was married for a long time but lost his wife five or six years ago. Cancer, I think. I've seen him around town with girlfriends before, but not for a while now."

"Wow, that's too bad about his wife," I said. "I'm sure that's rough, going through something like that."

"Shit happens," Kelly said in her lawyer voice. Couldn't argue with that lawyer logic. She was good. "Listen," she continued, "I actually called to see if you wanted to come over for a barbecue on Sunday afternoon. Ben is going to fix up some ribs and a nice batch of grilled veggies."

"Ooh, that sounds, great. I'd love to! Thanks for the invite!" I said, glad for the subject change. I usually went down to OKC to have dinner with my parents on Sundays, but I figured they could muddle through without me for one week.

"Want me to bring my secret family-recipe cheesecake?" I asked, already knowing I probably only got invited because they wanted cheesecake and were luring me in with the prospect of barbecue.

"Yes please," she said quickly. "And beer."

"Of course."

"Oh, and feel free to bring a friend," she added.

"Right."

"Good luck," she said.

"With the cheesecake?" I asked, knowing full well that wasn't what she meant.

"No, Bev, with the article. Or the stakeout. Or both. In either case, it's a good thing we had you sign your trust documents last month. I'll take care of the chickens if Bigfoot gets you or if Mark kills you for turning in a crappy article. Yeah, either way, I'll take the chickens." I knew she only wanted them so that her husband could barbecue them all.

"Thanks, you're a true friend." She only loved me for my cheesecake and my chickens, I thought sullenly.

We hung up, and I flat out gave up on the article, opting

for bed instead. As I lay in bed trying to fall asleep, a million things raced through my mind. I hoped that Beryl was okay out there, wherever she was. I thought about Danny. My rational brain was not 100 percent convinced that Kelly had provided sufficient proof of his relationship status. It seemed to always be looking for excuses. But anyway, why did I care one way or another? I regretted asking her. It's just that the conversation I'd overheard at the *Ledger* between Danny and Mark had gotten me thinking. Then I thought about him losing his wife, and I felt sad. So I changed up my thoughts. I imagined writing a bad romance novel about it. I pictured a silk negligee-wearing hot soccer mom divorcée, saving the neighbor widower from a life of loneliness and grief by bringing him cheesecakes and offering to mop his kitchen. Some people dealt with the tough things in life with shopping or therapy; I used bad romance novel plot ideas.

When I did finally get to sleep, it was a fitful sort of slumber, full of dreams of Danny's face morphing into—you guessed it—Sasquatch. While Mark was yelling at me to finish writing an article about cheesecake.

FIFTEEN

I woke up early Friday morning, the sunlight and the peace-fulness of the crisp morning air a welcomed change from the supreme weirdness of my dream world. I was feeling anxious, though, and thought maybe a run would help get rid of some of the nervous energy that had built up over the week. If I didn't get rid of it, it might get ugly. For Guthrie.

On my way out of the house, I stopped by the coop. The chickens seemed glad to see me, which I thought was weird until I remembered that Beryl wasn't there. It was as if they were already happier without her. I still felt bad. Maybe I'd see her when I went on my run, and as I made my way along my neighborhood route, I looked for her the whole way. I almost tripped three times, but it was to no avail. No Beryl anywhere. I just hoped her end had been a swift, painless one. If she had been taken in by someone, I wished them better luck than I had with her.

I had a little breakfast and coffee after my shower, checked back in on the remaining birds, and took the car to work. But instead of turning off the engine in a parking space in front of The Book Store, I found myself turning off the engine in a parking space in front of Missy's Bakery. It always seemed to happen when I drove to work, which probably was why I tried to walk most days.

As I waited in line to order my workout prize, I looked around at the other people in the bakery. Parents with their kids, older folks with their grandkids. Hipsters with beanies. One of Mark's friends, Max, was sitting at a table with his wife and their son. He waved hello to me, and I smiled and waved back. I recognized a few other people in the shop and exchanged more smiles and hellos while I waited. In that moment, I felt like I belonged, and in that moment, I had an actual answer for that question of why I moved here. I moved here to feel this way—like a normal person, doing normal things, in a small town where the pace of life was a little slower and a little sweeter, donuts notwithstanding. I felt content, and I felt like I was home. It was something I had never felt in Manhattan. I loved it.

I ordered a chocolate buttermilk donut and a coffee. Lord knew I didn't need any more caffeine today, but what the hell. It went well with the donut. As I stood and watched the woman behind the counter put my donut in a bag, I had a thought. My warm and fuzzy "I am home" feeling suddenly turned into one of doom and gloom. I wondered if everyone else in the shop believed in Bigfoot and I was the only one who didn't. The odds were definitely against me.

I collected my booty and drove to the shop where I devoured my delicious donut and drank my coffee much too quickly. When my phone read ten o'clock, I unlocked the front door and proceeded to send a business-related text.

Me: *Good morning, Danny—it's Beverley Green.*

Danny: *Hey, how's things?*

I was curious to see how chatty he would be. Was he asking me how things were because he really wanted to know? Or was this a standard greeting-type thing? How should I answer? Should I tell him I just ate a really delicious donut? Or should I skip right to the point? And why was I worrying about something this stupid? Oh right. The extra cup of coffee.

I hated texting someone I didn't know well. But not as much as I hated the prospect of calling Danny about this particular subject.

Me: *Pretty good... you?*

Danny: *About the same! What's up?*

Me: *So, does your offer to help me with my article still stand?*

Danny: *Sure! What did you have in mind?*

Me: *Are you busy tomorrow?*

And just like that, we had made plans to meet up at the *Ledger* building around eight the following night so that he could take me on my very first personal, official Bigfoot stake-out. And if I thought this article was stressing me out before, it turned out that was all just peanuts compared to now. I made a quick list of things to consider and then spent the rest of the morning freaking out about the items on my list. Minus the doodles and a few hundred exclamation marks, my list looked like this:

BIGFOOT STAKE-OUT

1. What do I wear?

2. Do I need a gun?

3. !!!DON'T FORGET BREATH MINTS!!!

4. Conversation starters? (Index cards?)

5. DON'T FORGET COFFEE

6. What if I actually see Bigfoot?!?!

7. First aid kit

8. Put safe deposit box key somewhere where Kelly will find it

9. What am I thinking

I considered calling Kelly to tell her what I was going to do, but perhaps sometimes Bigfoot stakeouts were better left to oneself. Or was this a date? Oh my goodness. I was pretty sure it wasn't a date, but when I realized that it could possibly be construed as one, I added this worrying thought to my list as item number ten. Then I started freaking out about that, too.

10. OH MY GOD IS THIS A DATE?!!?

11. Seriously, don't forget breath mints

Could this really be considered a date? If so, it just might be the first time in history that a first date consisted of hiding in some bushes waiting for Sasquatch. But then again, given how weird people could be, maybe it wouldn't actually be the first time in human history. But it could definitely still be considered weird, and it was definitely a first for me. I'd had some weird first dates in my day, but none of them had gone anything like this.

So how was I supposed to dress for a Bigfoot stakeout that might also be a first date? No pressure here... I did a web search for "what to wear on a Bigfoot stakeout that might also be a first date" but didn't come up with anything usable. A search result did come up for "Bigfoot negligee," but I so did not want to go there.

Fortunately, my afternoon was quite busy, dealing with a surprise visit from a moms' group with their kids. It was a nice way to end the day, and the week.

SIXTEEN

ON SATURDAY MORNING I woke up slowly, keeping my eyes closed as I let my body wake up. I stretched and yawned and suddenly sat bolt upright in bed, eyes wide open. I looked at the time: 8:00. I had slept in later than I usually did. I had this feeling like maybe I was forgetting something. Wasn't there something I should be worrying about right now? Bigfoot? Yes, of course I should be worrying about Bigfoot. But it seemed like there was something else. Yes, I was pretty sure there was that other thing I should be bothered about. But what?

Was I supposed to be going to the bookstore early? No, I was having Julie work for me today. Sheesh! What could it have been. Sitting there in bed, I heard a series of soft clucks coming from the backyard. Oh. Right. The property manager was coming in two hours to make sure I didn't have any chickens. Wait, what? Oh shoot.

Before going into full panic mode, I took a few deep breaths and tried to think about what the next step should be, other than going into full panic mode. It probably should have something to do with getting up and getting dressed. Yes, that sounded good. Slowly and steadily, I climbed out of bed and looked for some clothes—something that wouldn't get ruined if it got covered in chicken poop. Better safe than sorry.

I walked outside, and everything seemed copacetic in the coop. Of course it was! The main troublemaker had, um, flown it. I stood and felt the cool Oklahoma morning air on my face and arms; it was lovely. I could handle this. I could figure out what to do. On the inside, I was running around the yard screaming my head off about getting evicted because I didn't know chickens weren't allowed in Guthrie. On the outside, I remained cool, calm, and confident I'd find a way to circumvent a really stupid law.

I heard more dub reggae coming from Zach and Zoe's backyard, and I smelled the herbage. They were getting an early start on their Saturday, it seemed. And then the light bulb went on, and I had my plan.

An hour and a half later, I was in my kitchen making myself a big giant Saturday breakfast—because heaven knew I both needed and deserved it—when there was a knock on the front door.

"Door's open," I yelled from the kitchen. I was reasonably sure it was Allan from Prairie Wind Property Management. It could have been Bigfoot, in which case I'd just invite him to breakfast for reals this time.

"Hello," I heard a man calling through the house. "It's Allan from Prairie Wind Property Management!"

Man, Bigfoot was good at impersonating real estate guys.

"Come on through," I called. A few seconds later a rotund, clean-shaven, tidily dressed man appeared in the doorway. He was in his midthirties, and his light brown hair was parted on the side and pulled across his head, like he was practicing for when he would go bald and he'd need to do the comb-over thing.

"Hi, you must be Beverley," he said as he walked into the room. "I'm Allan." He smiled and extended his hand to me, which held his business card. I almost laughed out loud; it seemed that every person in real estate was hell-bent on giving everyone else in the world a business card.

I took the card and didn't really want to shake his hand, but he kept it floating in front of me until I grabbed it and flopped it around a few times. I looked at his full name on the card: Allan Higgenbotham. Well, that sounded about right. "Hi, Allan," I said cordially. "I'm just making some breakfast —scrambled eggs, bacon, and hash browns. Want some? The eggs are super fresh," I added as an afterthought.

He looked at the pans on the stove longingly before answering. "Uh, no thanks. I um, had a Weight Watchers shake before I left the house." He closed his eyes and took a deep breath, as if he wanted to eat the air. He shook his head slightly, remembering he had better get back to business instead of dreaming about real food. He pushed his thick-framed glasses back up the bridge of his nose. "I can't stay long," he added with some sadness in his voice.

"Suit yourself. But if you don't mind, I'm going to eat. I'm starved!" I scooped a huge pile of food onto a plate and sat down at the kitchen table in front of a huge bowl of fruit. I truly was starved. Turned out hiding a brood of chickens was hard work. "Have a seat," I offered.

He pulled out a chair and sat down opposite me. He had a manila folder with him, which he placed on the table. He opened it up and carefully looked over the contents.

"So," he started, looking up just in time to watch me put a

ANDREA C. NEIL

giant forkful of eggs into my mouth. It was as if he was looking at me like I was a giant turkey drumstick, like in the cartoons we watched as kids. He was starting to make me a bit nervous.

"Yeah?" I asked with my mouth full of food.

"I'm here on behalf of your landlady, Mrs. Tisdale. She just wanted me to conduct an inspection of the property."

"Isn't that usually only done upon move-in and move-out?"

"Typically yes," he said, pushing up his glasses again. "But the property owner can request additional inspections, if the proper notice is given. It's all in the contract you signed. Would you like to read it?" He shuffled the papers around on the table.

"No, that's okay," I said, biting into a crispy piece of bacon. He was watching my every move again, and it was starting to feel like a weird type of food porn. Another topic that I would rather not explore in real life *or* in my novel writing. I decided to stop eating, no matter how hungry I still was, and wait until he had left before finishing my meal in private. "Well, inspect away, Allan." I wondered if that had been specific enough for him. "I mean the house, inspect the house," I added hastily. I was just making it worse. He either wasn't listening or did a great job ignoring me.

We stood up, and he looked intently around the room. Both of our gazes traveled to the window above the sink, out the window to the backyard, finally landing on the pristine, empty chicken coop.

"Can you tell me what you're looking for?" I asked, trying to sound both innocent and interested. I knew damn well what he was looking for, of course. Part of me was petrified that he'd find evidence of illegal chicken activity and evict me. That was the "law-abiding, upright citizen" part of me. Then there was another part of me, the rebellious "I don't give a rat's ass what people think of me" part, which was growing stronger day by day. And that part of me really didn't give a rat's ass whether this squishy guy found fresh chicken poop in my yard or not.

"Let's see here." He looked through his papers again as we stood at the table. "It says here that there is suspicion of avian animal husbandry on the premises." He looked around the kitchen again, as if he was expecting to find chickens roaming around under the table, looking for crumbs maybe.

I waved my arm through the air like Vanna White waving at a vowel. "Well, as you can see, Allan, the closest thing you'll find to a chicken in here is on my breakfast plate." I was proud of my funny, but I could tell from the blank expression on Allan's face that he was thoroughly unimpressed.

"Yes, yes, I can see that," he said slowly. "But if you don't mind, I'm just going to take a quick look around the rest of the property."

Hell yes I minded, but it wouldn't do any good to say so. I just shrugged and smiled before sitting back down in front of my food. It had all tasted extra delicious, and I wanted to get back to it. The eggs were, of course, from my chickens.

Just then, the sound of cackling chickens floated into the kitchen through the open window. I froze for a second, until I remembered that there were no longer any birds in my backyard, and the noise had come from the neighbors' house. I was pretty sure my lease contract didn't allow Mr. Higgenbotham to search my neighbors' house.

Allan stood up a little taller, pushed his glasses back up, and walked over to the window and peered out across the backyard. Just an empty chicken coop out there.

"Is that a chicken coop?" he asked.

"Is that what that thing is?" I pretended to be excited. "It was here when I moved in; I wasn't sure what it was for until just now! Really, that's a chicken coop?"

He turned around to look at me, his expression hurt that I was trying to bullshit him.

"I've been living in New York," I added quickly. "Manhattan. I guess I'm a city girl at heart—I don't know anything about this stuff!" I waved my fork at him and shrugged again. "A chicken coop. Well, whaddya know."

"Yes, well, I do believe that's what a structure like that is used for," Allan said. He looked through the papers in his folder again. "I don't see anything here about a coop being on the property when you moved in. And where are those, uh, chicken noises coming from?"

"What? Oh, you mean those weird clucky noises? God, I've been wondering all this time what those noises were. Chickens! Allan, you've been such a great help to me today!" I pointed towards my neighbors' house. "I think the noises are coming from next door. I thought maybe they just had a few interesting... well, you know, 'extracurricular activities' of some sort." I watched him blush.

He opened the back door and walked out onto the patio, and I followed him out. I'd had a few minutes before breakfast to clean out the chicken coop, so it kind of looked like it had been empty for a while, not just a few hours. I had suggested to Zach and Zoe that they lay off their extracurricular herbal intake until later in the morning but the animal noises from their yard were still coming over loud and clear. I continued playing dumb.

"So are chickens not allowed or something?" I put my hand on my hip and threw it out to the side, accentuating my curves. I figured that couldn't hurt anything—except my back. If necessary I was also prepared to start eating hash browns in front of him. "What's all the fuss about, anyway?"

He eyed my hip suspiciously before speaking. "According to city bylaws, raising chickens or other domesticated farm animals is not allowed in residential neighborhoods." He sounded like he was quoting the law verbatim. I wagered he could also give me the ordinance number. Or bylaw number. Or whatever it was called. I bet I could ask him what it was called, and he would know. I could tell Allan knew all about this kind of stuff.

"Oh, really? Wow, that's very interesting. I wonder if my neighbors know that. I've never met them before, but maybe I should let them know," I said thoughtfully.

"If you like, I can go over there," Allan suggested.

"Oh no, that's okay. I mean, really, it's none of our business, anyway, is it? I'll let them know, and like, break it to them gently. I think they're elderly; I'm sure they just don't know the rules."

"Okay then," he said doubtfully.

We walked back into the kitchen, and I offered to give Allan a tour of the rest of the house. I stopped in each room, pointing out all the improvements I had made, including nice new paint (all neutral colors of course), some new bathroom fixtures, and even a new ceiling fan in the bedroom. He seemed pleased. I explained how I did the work myself, and how I loved the natural light of the house, and how Leona Tisdale was such a lovely human.

I ended our tour at the front door and opened it to show him how I'd even lubricated the lock.

"Well, Miss Green, you've kept the place in outstanding condition. I'm sure Mrs. Tisdale will be pleased."

"Oh, I do hope so, Allan," I said sweetly. "I hope you'll give me a glowing review." I showed him out the front door.

"I certainly will!"

"All right, thank you! And be sure to let me know if there's anything else I can do, okay? Stop by the bookstore sometime!" Oh dear. I didn't know Allan's relationship status, but I hoped he didn't think I was interested in him. I couldn't be sure, the way he had been leering at my bacon earlier.

He waved to me before getting into his Oldsmobile and driving away.

Crisis averted! For now. On to the next one.

SEVENTEEN

AFTER I POLITELY SENT MR. HIGGENBOTHAM ON his way, I went over to Zach and Zoe's to retrieve my chickens. I promised them that I'd buy them some good imported beer as a thank-you for saving my butt. I made a mental note to grab some for them when I went out later to get some for Kelly's barbecue. If you drank alcohol in Oklahoma, you really had to plan ahead, because you couldn't buy any wine, real beer, or other spirits on Sundays. Oklahomans thought buying alcohol on Sunday made you immoral. More immoral than we already were Monday through Saturday, that is. And maybe it did, but I was already a lost cause, so I was all for repealing a law that had probably been on the books since 1907 when Oklahoma became a state.

I was in dire need of a shower, and once that was done, I resumed freaking out about going Bigfoot hunting on what could be considered a first date with a very good-looking man. I started rooting through my closet in earnest, because I hadn't yet answered the number one question on my Bigfoot Stakeout To-Do List: what to wear.

I did manage to find some jeans and an NYU sweatshirt that would probably work just fine. But I decided that the occasion called for new shoes. Boots. Maybe cowboy boots. I didn't have any, and I thought maybe I should have some. I mean, that's what you did when you lived in Oklahoma, right? I was pretty sure I had owned some in high school. Anyway, it was a great excuse to procrastinate some more—and have lunch in Edmond for a change of scenery.

I got in my car and drove the twenty-five minutes down to Tener's Western Outfitters to see what the latest and greatest was in ladies' boot fashion. But when I got there and started walking down the aisles, my eyes glazed over. Square-toed? Pointy? Ropers? Fringe? All the colors and the fancy stitching was starting to make me anxious. Maybe I just needed food. I hightailed it out of there and found a pho restaurant right down the street. As I ate I realized that maybe it wasn't the boots that had me feeling anxious; maybe it had been low blood sugar. But I couldn't be sure, so I decided to put off buying any fancy shoes. My Vans would do just fine for Bigfoot scouting. It was probably easier to run for my life in Vans than boots, anyway.

I hit some traffic on the way back, due to some construction on I-35. At one point, two lanes merged down to one, slowing things way down. Getting stuck in traffic was one occasion where the New Yorker in me definitely won out, and I found myself getting frustrated and impatient as I waited for my turn to merge with cars in the other lane. Not to mention I had wasted several hours on a useless boot-shopping trip when I should have been writing, or fixing my hair.

I merged lanes and my car inched forward toward the construction zone. It was state law to merge as soon as a sign told you to, but of course there were plenty of people who ignored the rule and sped all the way up to the merge site and forced their way in front of everyone else who had patiently complied with the law. As I watched this happen, it made me even more mad. Being late and feeling rushed was not how I wanted to feel while preparing for the night's activities. I got lost in frustration and Bigfoot anxiety, and before I knew it a big giant white truck had sped up next to me and then almost stopped. It had black, mean-looking wheels and giant rearview mirrors that extended out about six feet out from the side of the truck, and the whole thing appeared to be three times as tall as my reasonably-sized Subaru. Why did people feel compelled to drive something that damn big? Sure, there were maybe a few people who actually needed vehicles that big, on a ranch or for construction or something equally as rough and rugged. But I guessed that at least 90 percent of people who drove those things were just people trying to prove something to the world. Most likely, I reckoned they were trying to prove that they were asshats.

The driver of this particular vehicle was trying to cut the line and get in front of me. He hadn't merged when he was supposed to, like the law said to. Nope, he had zoomed all the way to the front of the line and was now expecting me to let him in. It was assumed that if I didn't let him in, he'd use his fifty-foot tall truck to make a Subaru pancake out of me. I happened to be riding the bumper of the car in front of me, because that was just the kind of driver I was, especially when I could feel it in my bones that a big giant truck was going to try to cut me off. He could damn well try his luck with the person behind me. Why did people who drove big giant trucks drive like this? Oh right—two reasons. One, because they were usually asshats. And two, because they could. Well, I wasn't going to let this jerk get in front of me. I kept as close to the car in front of me as I could without giving its driver some sort of intimate medical exam, while the truck kept on coming to my right. I looked straight ahead and set my jaw.

Maybe it was all the carbs in the pho noodles. Maybe it was the fact that I was running late, or that in just a matter of hours, I was not going to be able to outrun my fear of Bigfoot any longer. Or maybe it was simply that drivers of big giant trucks were aggressive meanies, but next thing I knew, I heard a terrible scraping sound and my car started to shudder. I looked over to my right and was eye-level with the lower half of the truck's driver's-side door. He was simply pushing me out of the way.

I was so pissed and so frustrated and riding an adrenaline and pho noodle high, that I just reset my jaw and kept on driving. The driver of the giant truck of death finally slowed, got in line behind me, and then got off at the next exit. He was probably scared I was going to stop and kick his ass. Yes, that was probably why he did that. I won! I just kept on driving. If Bigfoot ended up killing me and eating me for a midnight snack, a smashed-up car would be the least of my worries.

I didn't stop to look at my poor car until I got all the way home and pulled into my driveway. I hadn't been able to see any visible damage in my side-view mirror, but I was dreading getting out and looking. Did I have giant Shesquatch-type fingernail scratches down the side of my car? Was I going to have to replace two doors or a few tires or wheels? I hadn't needed to stop on the way home because of a flat tire, so that was a good sign. I got out and walked around to the other side of my car. And lo and behold, all I could see was a few minor scratches in the door bumper guard thingies

(I have a great vocabulary, but not when it comes to car parts). They could probably be buffed out. It was a true miracle. As I walked inside, I silently promised myself to be a nicer driver. If only big giant truck asshat drivers would do the same.

I rebalanced my energy by having a little snack, this time opting for more protein because hello! Brain food. I realized I had a little bit of time to do some writing, so I continued on a very vague outline for my article, hoping against all odds that I would gain enough insight and material that night to finish the damn thing the next day. I kept yawning, though, so I took a quick catnap. It seemed like a real possibility that I might be up all night, and maybe it would be a good idea to be awake enough that I could hold a conversation with my safari guide. Or at least be coherent when Sasquatch gnawed my foot off. Needless to say, I didn't sleep well.

I was nervous about the evening—apprehensive about going monster hunting and concerned that I'd be able to look fabulous while I did it. Or at least not look like a terrified idiot. What would it be like spending the night heaven knows where with Danny? Did I trust him? Wait, what did that mean, did I trust him? Did I expect him to protect me from Bigfoot, or to act like a gentleman? I found myself kind of hoping he didn't act like a complete gentleman. But at the same time, I didn't really want him to be too distracted from protecting me against Bigfoot. Such are the dilemmas of the modern woman. I made a quick mental note of that last phrase, thinking it might make a good tag line for a romance novel. Or my memoir.

As evening approached, I put some provisions together for the stakeout. I grabbed my backpack and threw in a flash-light, my reporter's notebook plus one blank notebook (you never knew when writing inspiration might hit), a few pens, and an old can of mace I'd had in my apartment in Manhattan since 2006. Then I brewed a big batch of coffee in my Chemex and put it in my forty-ounce thermos. Thank goodness I had a very large backpack, because I wasn't even close to being done gathering supplies. I also put in a full tin of Altoids, a few protein bars, a ham sandwich, some tortilla chips, and two apples. Plus a bar of dark chocolate and a hefty stash of cookies from Trader Joe's that my parents had brought me. If I was about to get taken out by a big furry monster, I was going to do it after dessert.

When I was packed, repacked, and otherwise ready, I added one more ham sandwich to my bulging backpack (I didn't want to be rude and not have one to offer Danny). I put on my stakeout outfit and drove over to the *Ledger* building. I was nervous, for so many different reasons. Neither a date nor a possible encounter with Bigfoot ever gave me cause for anxiety in New York. I was losing my touch.

EIGHTEEN

"Toughen up, Beverley!" I muttered to myself as I parked in front of the *Ledger* building. I looked up and down my side of the street, and it was empty; mine was the only car around. I looked over at my giant backpack and regretted not having put a flask of whiskey in it. I started to worry I'd either gotten stood up or had gotten the time of our meeting wrong.

Just then I heard a car door close. I checked my rearview mirror, and across the street behind me, Danny was standing in front of a big, giant white truck, smiling. Oh. My. God. Was that *the* truck? The one that had tried to run me over earlier on I-35? It couldn't have been. Surely Danny wouldn't drive like that. But I never saw the driver of that big white tank, so I had to admit it could have been him. I started to sweat. I took a deep breath, grabbed my overstuffed bag, and got out of my car.

He started walking across the street to meet me. "Hi," he said in a deeper voice than I remembered.

"Hi," I said in a voice that was several octaves higher than my usual one. I tried to smile. Unsuccessfully.

"Here, let me take that." He nodded at my bag and reached out to take it. Before I could protest, he had lifted it out of my hands. "Shit!" he exclaimed as he tried to steady himself. It seemed to be a little heavier than he had been anticipating.

"I came prepared," I admitted sheepishly.

"For what, Armageddon?"

"Maybe." If there was an Armageddon, it was a pretty sure bet that there would be Bigfeet involved.

He shook his head as we walked across the street.

"You're kind of an aggressive driver, aren't you!" he continued as we walked toward his car.

Oh dear. Had he recognized me from the Highway Incident? Now I was even more afraid that it had been him. I tried to look a little closer at his truck to see if I could recognize anything about it. It did have black wheels. And it was very large. But beyond that, I couldn't really be sure, it had all happened so fast. Regardless, I wondered what he was trying to prove, driving such a huge vehicle. Was he an asshat like the rest of them? I really hoped it hadn't been him.

"Why would you say that?" I asked, trying to sound as innocent as I could.

He walked me to the passenger door of the truck and opened it for me. "I was following you down the street just now. You took the corners pretty fast and whipped right into that spot. Were you afraid you'd be late or something?" I wasn't looking at him, but I could feel him about to break into a laugh. I looked for a good foothold someplace on the truck and hoisted myself up and in. It was like automotive mountain climbing.

I shrugged again. "Habit." Since I was still a little scared that he was actually referring to my driving earlier in the day, I figured the less I said the better.

"What do you have in this thing exactly?" he asked as he handed my bag up to me.

"Provisions," I answered flatly.

He walked around to the other side and got in, and off we went. He turned north onto Division Street. It seemed like we were taking up two lanes of traffic in his gigantic vehicle, and we were high enough up that I felt like I was in a small plane.

"Does this thing need clearance from air traffic control?" I asked.

Danny laughed. "It is kind of obnoxious, isn't it? I usually just keep it for working around the ranch. Normally I wouldn't drive this thing around town, but my other vehicle is in the shop, and well, since we're kind of headed off-road, I thought it would be okay."

I nodded silently. "What is your other car?" I was curious but also sort of afraid to hear the answer.

"A Land Rover."

"Oh." I was kind of disappointed as that would have been the perfect safari vehicle. Well, maybe next time.

We continued driving north and west, heading out of Guthrie. I hadn't been up this direction much; I'd never had a reason to. I couldn't picture what was around. "So where are we headed?" I asked.

"I thought we'd head toward my place," he answered.

I nodded silently again. I watched the scenery go by in the late-evening light. The sun was setting, and it would be gone below the horizon soon. There was a thick layer of clouds along the western skyline, providing plenty of material for an amazing sunset. The light reflected off the clouds and created a million different shades of pink, orange, yellow, and red. Oklahoma really knew how to do sunsets, there was no denying it.

I knew that we were both admiring the scenery, but there was some tension in the air. It was like the idea of going to "his place" somehow made me more nervous. Usually those words had certain... implications. Usually having to do with something less scary, and often times more fun, than seeing Bigfoot. I felt like I was in high school again. Okay, maybe actually college. I was a late bloomer.

There was no music playing in the truck; the only sound was that of the oversized tires barreling down the road. I was so nervous that I wasn't sure how to start talking without betraying just how scared I really was. But I also figured I needed to say something to break the silence. Most of the time, I was one of those people who felt like I had to fill empty spaces with words. This was one of those times.

"I really appreciate you helping me out," I said. Lame.

"Oh, it's no problem at all!" he said quickly, probably as grateful as me to have a conversation going. He sounded suspiciously happy about going on a Bigfoot search, though. "I'm glad you took me up on my offer. This will be cool! I hope you're ready for some fun."

I looked at him, silently thinking, man, you have a really twisted idea of what fun is. He looked me, his eyebrows raised and a big grin flashing his perfect teeth at me. He looked genuinely excited. It was cute.

"Sure!" I answered. I tried my best to sound excited, but I probably sounded like I did when my insurance agent would ask me if I wanted to go ahead and schedule an appointment to go over my liability policy. If my insurance agent was half as cute as Danny was, I probably would own a lot more insurance policies.

I wasn't entirely convinced that the evening would actually qualify as "fun," but everybody had their own unique definition of the word, and I certainly couldn't deny him of his. However weird it was. I just hoped that tonight, "fun" didn't involve things like death, big sharp fangs, dismemberment, or abductions. I started to nod silently again, my head bobbing up and down, still trying to convince itself that yeah! This was fun.

We drove for about ten minutes more, which seemed much longer since I was still struggling with how to keep the conversation going. On the opposite side of the sky as the sunset, the moon was almost full, which would help illuminate the landscape a little bit as it got darker. I still couldn't make out any familiar landmarks and eventually gave up trying. I was glad that it wasn't a new moon—that would have meant it would have been pitch effing black out there, and the night would have been that much scarier.

Danny slowed his truck, and we turned onto a one-lane road. It was a private road—so the sign said—and I guessed we were on his property. He'd said he owned a ranch, but I wasn't sure how people defined "ranch" out here, so I had no idea what to expect.

We passed a large stone house with a three-car garage on the side. I couldn't see a whole lot of details in the growing darkness, but it looked like a really nice place. The walkway leading to the front door was illuminated by garden lights, revealing some nice landscaping in the yard and around the house. It was a fairly modern-looking homestead: clean lines, no frill, but at the same time not too austere, either. I wondered if there was a pool.

"So this is your place?" I asked as we drove past the house and back into the darkness. The paved road ended just then and was replaced by a gravel one.

"Yep," he answered casually. "We're headed toward the back of the property. I think we'll have a pretty good chance of seeing something out that way."

Oh. Right. I'd sort of forgotten for a few minutes why we were there. I was kind of disappointed that he hadn't forgotten. Because if he hadn't, I could have imagined that we were heading out for a piece of pie and a cup of coffee or something really innocent like that.

"Do you have a pool?" I asked before my brain even had a fighting chance of trying to stop my mouth. I had been wanting to make a friend in town who had a pool so I could invite myself over during those long, steamy summer months to dive into a cool, refreshing giant water puddle. I was mildly excited by the prospect of him having a pool, but I didn't want it to sound like I was already inviting myself over quite yet. Bigfoot first, then pool.

"Yep, there's one out back behind the house," he answered. I thought I detected an air of wistfulness in his voice. I wondered if he had maybe built the pool for someone else, for a life that he no longer had due to circumstances that had been out of his control. "Why do you ask? Want to use it sometime?" He looked at me and raised his eyebrows expectantly. He seemed a little less wistful at that point. I could picture him trying to picture me in my swimsuit, and I didn't mind all that much.

"I was just wondering," I replied innocently. "It looks like a nice house."

"It works."

It was even darker now, and the vegetation along the

sides of the road seemed more dense. Trees lined the road and had grown over the top of it, creating a canopy that was probably beautiful in the daylight but almost impossible to see now. It felt like we were in a cave, headed deep into the jungle on our Bigfoot Safari. I double-checked the window to make sure it was rolled all the way up.

"Where are we headed exactly?" I asked as the road turned from bumpy gravel to bumpy dirt. My anxiety was growing.

"We're going to the very back of the property," he said, squinting out the window. Then he turned down an even bumpier, dirtier road. "Here we are!" he said a few minutes later as we reached the end of the road—literally and figuratively. We were in a small clearing. He put the truck in park and turned off the engine. The headlights went dark, leaving us sitting in total blackness. I was unsure of what came next. Was this it? Were we going to sit right here all night? Was it safe? Where was the bathroom?

"Let me just check my messages real quick. Reception isn't very good out there." He got out his phone and turned it on. The screen lit up his handsome features, and I watched him as he began typing a message. "I was waiting to hear back on a piece of property," he mumbled as he got lost in his task.

As I watched him, I considered the huge disparity between the two major issues I had with this whole newspaper article. On the one hand, I didn't believe in Bigfoot. There was just no way this kind of thing existed. We can find a thousand different types of moths, but we can't prove the existence of a giant furry man monster? It just didn't sit right. At the same time, I was petrified of the thought of actually seeing one. But I couldn't have it both ways. Either I believed it existed, and I was admitting I might actually see one in person tonight, or I didn't believe in them and they were fake like I had been insisting all along—in which case, I had nothing to worry about. So which was it? It was time to choose. Was I going to approach this as a hoax or as a woman scared out of her mind that she would be ravaged in the forest by Sasquatch?

Maybe I could still try to play both sides here, I thought. Maybe I didn't actually have to choose yet. I decided to continue traveling down the middle path. I would remain very, very skeptical, while still allowing myself to be scared of monsters. Was this being indecisive? No. This was being smart.

Thankfully my circular thoughts were interrupted by Danny's smooth voice. He had finished up on his phone and was ready to go. "Let's go find us a Sasquatch!" he exclaimed with way too much enthusiasm.

"Okay," I said with much, much less enthusiasm.

NINETEEN

DANNY JUMPED out of the truck and came around to the passenger side, swinging his backpack gracefully across one shoulder. I'd gotten the passenger door open but was trying to figure out how to get out of the truck without being taken down by my own backpack in the process. I didn't see any ropes with which I could rappel down the side, and I was feeling stuck. Just then he reached for my bag and then my hand, helping me down to lower altitude.

"Do you actually find it helpful to have this thing so high up off the ground?" I asked.

"Oh, I don't know," he confessed. "It seemed like the thing to do. Plus it annoys the hell out of people in traffic."

"I'll bet it does!" I exclaimed, still playing innocent. "I don't exactly have a tiny car or anything, but when I get behind one of you guys, I can't see a damn thing."

He laughed. "I thought you would like my big, manly truck." He extended his arm, gesturing for me to take the lead as we started walking toward a barely perceptible opening in the tree line, about ten yards from the front bumper of his ManMobile.

"I always thought men who drove big giant trucks were trying too hard to prove something, and that it usually had something to do with proving the, um, large dimensions of their manhood. But usually it ended up being a statement about their lack thereof."

He laughed even harder. "Are you saying I'm trying to compensate for something? You sound like a cross between a librarian and a psychologist."

I had to laugh, too. "Thank you," I boasted. I knew he was poking fun at me, but I'd rather sound like a librarian and a psychologist than, say, a politician and a proctologist.

"I was going to ask you what you might infer about *my* manhood based on this truck, but now I don't think I want to know. However, I can assure you, Miss Green, that in this particular case, the vehicle happens to be a very accurate representation of the dimensions of the owner's manhood." He had such confidence in his voice that I didn't doubt him in the least. Just three seconds of thinking about it set my cheeks on fire, and I knew my face was a nice tomato red. Thank god we were walking in darkness.

I took a deep breath and tried to let the cool night air clear the color from my cheeks. All I could do was try for a subject change.

"There is no way I'm taking the lead into that jungle," I protested as we came to the tree line. I stopped and turned to look at him. I hoped my face wasn't still red. His was a perfect shade of cute.

"Okay." He puffed up his chest a little, rising to the occasion. He shot me a sparkly look before turning and walking into the trees.

"Hey, wait!" I called after him. I said a silent prayer and followed him in.

We walked a narrow path, neither of us talking anymore. I wondered if it was because we were trying to be stealthy or because we just didn't have anything to say to each other. In my case, I was too unnerved to form coherent sentences.

It was colder now that the sun had been down a while, and I zipped my hoodie up a little farther as we walked. I was glad I had brought it. I wasn't sure how long we would be outside, and I started to regret not bringing a hat. I realized I didn't do as good of a job packing for my Sasquatch retreat as I had thought. I might not starve to death with all my snacks, but I could imagine getting dragged into the wilderness and dying of hypothermia.

After walking for what seemed like days, we came to a small clearing, at the edge of which stood a small cabin. It was a simple wooden structure—nothing fancy, but not exactly a shack, either. There was a small porch along the front, with a bench under one large window. Danny walked up to the door and unlocked it, waiting for me to catch up. I was about to walk in when he leaned over, reached an arm in front of me and then inside the cabin, and flipped on a light switch. He saw my eyebrows raise in surprise as he invaded my personal space.

"Just turning on the light," he said, stifling a laugh. I shot him a look and walked in. "Kind of touchy today, huh? Oh wait, you've been kind of touchy every time I've seen you."

I was about to launch into an angry speech about how stupid that was, but for once I thought before I spoke and realized he was kind of right. Whether I had food on my face, or had just dropped my coffee, or was about to be dinner for Bigfoot, he seemed to catch me when I was most perturbed.

And he possibly may have even caught me when I was being a jerk on the freeway. Why would this nice person want to spend any time with me if I was always such a beyatch? I softened the look on my face and vowed to lighten up and try to be more jovial. Okay, maybe jovial was a stretch, but I could at least be less defensive.

"Sorry I'm a little on edge," I admitted as we walked into the cabin. "It's the whole 'I'm mortally terrified of Bigfoot' thing."

"I get that," Danny said calmly as he closed and locked the door. He poised his hand over the light switch on the wall. "Can you turn that lamp on?" he asked, pointing to a small reading lamp by a large comfy chair.

I did as he asked, and he turned the overhead light off. It was much darker in the room now, but lit by a softer, warmer light. I took a look around at our surroundings. We had entered into a large room that served as a kitchen, eating area, and living room. From what I could tell, there was maybe one bedroom and a bathroom down a short hallway in the back, and that was it. The walls and floor were bare wood, and there were two oversized chairs and a small coffee table centered around a fireplace on the wall opposite the kitchen. It looked cozy. Like, it would have been a nice place to stay while doing anything other than what we were actually there for.

"These are fancy digs for a stakeout," I commented.

"We could have used a hunting stand out by the lake, but I thought you might be a little more comfortable here. It's starting to get cooler at night. We'll be able to see fine, if this goes like I think it will."

Then I remembered why we were here. I mean, really

remembered. I started to sweat again. I looked closely at the door to make sure it was securely locked. But at the same time, I also wanted to be sure I could get out. I didn't really know Danny, and here I was placing my life in his hands. Would there be more threat from outside the cabin or from inside? Was Danny more dangerous than Bigfoot? Surely I was just being overly paranoid. All those cautionary tales my parents tried to use on me to get me to carry my can of mace in my purse were finally taking hold. I tried to banish the paranoid thoughts from my mind. He was best friends with Mark, and even Kelly vouched for him. But still, I hoped the GPS was working on my phone in case this turned out to be a cabin of death and I got trapped and someone would need to come look for my carcass.

I sat down in one of the comfy chairs, noting that it felt as comfy as it looked. I noticed two rifles next to the door in a gun rack that had been mounted on the wall. He saw me looking at them.

"That lake I mentioned isn't far from here. This place gets used for hunting trips sometimes, or as a guest house. It hasn't been used much lately, but I had it prepared for tonight." He bent down and lit two pillar candles that were on the coffee table. They made a nice warm light. Romantic almost. Almost.

"Prepared how?" I asked, watching the flickering candle flames. Did that mean clean sheets on the bed? Or a fresh can of pretzels in the pantry? Or both? The candles seemed overkill for a hunting shack.

"Oh, I just had it cleaned. It gets pretty dusty in here, especially when it sits empty for a while." He walked to the kitchen and checked the pantry. "And I had some snacks brought over. I know how you like to eat." His shoulders hunched up a little, like he was expecting me to throw something at him. I had actually thought about it.

Just then we heard a sound from outside the cabin. It wasn't very loud, but it was a distinct rustling sound. I froze, and Danny stood up a little taller, listening intently.

"What was that?" I whispered. "What do we do?" I eyed the guns on the wall. My stomach tensed up.

We heard the noise again, and Danny looked at his watch before slowly making his way to the window. He pulled the heavy curtain aside about an inch and looked out at the clearing. "Ah, it's nothing," he said, still looking out the window. "It's just a raccoon." He walked away from the window and sat down in the other chair.

"How will we know if Bigfoot is out there if we're sitting here relaxing by candlelight?" I asked, a bit nervously. "Will he knock on the door to let us know he's stopping by?"

Danny looked at me and shot me an exasperated look. "Clearly you haven't been hunting before," he declared. I wondered what exactly had given me away.

He walked over to the kitchen again, picked up a small laptop from the counter, and brought it back to his chair. He opened the computer up and fiddled with it for a minute or two. "Here we go!" he exclaimed. He put it on the coffee table and moved his chair so it was closer to mine. "Look," he said, picking up the laptop and showing it to me. On the screen, a grainy black-and-white video was running. It showed a clearing, surrounded by trees.

"Is this a new series on Netflix?" I had no idea what I was looking at.

"It's what's going on right outside the front door," he answered, like I was a real doofus. I couldn't blame him. "We just listen for different sounds and keep an eye on this." He set the laptop on the table in front of us and leaned back in his chair. "Now, I think we need some coffee, don't you?" He eyed my backpack. He knew me better than I thought.

We rifled through my bag and finally found the thermos of coffee. I poured some into two mugs Danny had retrieved from the kitchen, and we sat drinking the hot, strong coffee.

"This is really good," he said as he smelled the steam coming off the top of his second cup. "But I'd expect nothing less. I've heard you're a coffee connoisseur."

"From who?" I couldn't remember ever talking to Mark about coffee.

"A little bird." He smiled.

Damn that Bill Turner.

"Yes, well, it's true. I do like coffee. It's all about quality, not quantity," I assured him. I got up from my chair and walked to the window. I wanted to look outside, but I was too scared.

"Does Bigfoot know how to use power tools?" I asked.

Danny had taken another sip of coffee but almost choked on it. "Excuse me?" he half laughed, half sputtered.

"Does Bigfoot know how to use power tools," I repeated. "Or how about gardening equipment? Shovels? Axes? Large kitchen spoons?" I wondered how sophisticated Bigfoot was. I wanted to know what we were up against.

"You know, I'm really not sure. As far as I know, they only use their hands to—"

In all actuality, I really didn't want to hear the rest of that sentence. So I cut him off. "How can you be so sure we'll even see one tonight?" Even though I was enjoying myself so far, I just couldn't stop being afraid. I was petrified there was a cryptid eavesdropping right outside the front door. If we were quiet, I reckoned we'd be able to hear him mouth-breathing. I must have looked really nervous now, because Danny laughed at me. Again.

"Well, I put some snacks outside in that clearing," he admitted.

"That clearing right out there?" I jerked my thumb toward the door.

"Yup."

"Right outside this door."

"Right out there." He was really enjoying this.

"What kind of snacks?"

"Hostess Cupcakes. For some strange reason, they love those things. Don't ask me how I know."

"Okay," I answered. I hadn't planned on asking.

"Don't worry, I'm not part Sasquatch," he chided. "You can check my birth certificate."

I smiled. He was really trying to make me feel better. He got up and walked over to the window to stand next to me and reached out to move the curtain aside. He was so close I could detect a faint whiff of clean soap smell. My breath caught in my throat. It smelled so manly. And clean.

"It's okay," he said softly as he peered outside. "I'll protect you." He turned to look at me, and we were so close that when I looked into his blue eyes I almost fell into them. He smelled so nice. I decided to go sit back down before I started swooning. I checked the video feed from the clearing. Nothing.

He sat back down, too, and we made quiet small talk for a while, sometimes stopping to listen to a noise from outside. They were all false alarms, but I jumped every time. Finally he reached into his bag and pulled out a flask, offering it to me. I gladly accepted. Great minds think alike; greater minds remember to actually pack the flask.

"So," he said, "Be-ver-ley." He pronounced each syllable slowly.

"Dan-ny," I responded.

"Your name."

"What about it?"

"It's kind of old-fashioned, isn't it? I mean, you're not actually like, eighty or something, are you?" He took another swig from the flask before passing it back to me.

"What can I say," I sighed. "My parents are old-fashioned. They still think their 1982 touch-tone house phone is a technological miracle."

He laughed loudly. I couldn't tell if he thought I was really that funny or if he'd just been hitting the flask a little harder than I was.

"It's a family name," I continued. "It was my maternal grandmother's name. I know it's old-fashioned. Hell, it's just plain old. But it's me." I shrugged and took another swig myself. "And I loved that old broad," I said quietly, referring to my MeeMo.

"Well, I like it," he decided.

"What, this hooch?" I held up the flask. Maybe I should slow down a little, too.

"No, your name." He stood up again to look out the window one more time.

I rifled through my two-ton backpack again, this time pulling out a ham sandwich. I should probably put some actual food in my stomach with all the alcohol. I took out half and held it out to Danny. "You want?"

He walked back to take it, then sat down heavily in his chair. "Thanks," he said and started eating. "This is delicious!" he exclaimed. "Seriously, this is so damn good." He inhaled the rest of his half. "What's in this thing?"

"The number one key to happiness in life," I confided to him with my mouth full of sandwich, "is to never *ever* skimp on the mayo."

"Well, I'm a believer," he said happily, brushing a few crumbs off his shirt. Right then I knew that this man was real relationship material. I could never love a man who didn't love mayo.

It was his turn to share again; he leaned over and pulled something out of his bag, tossing it to me. A package of Hostess Cupcakes. "No sense in Sasquatch getting all the good snacks," he reasoned. We both started laughing as we pulled the crinkly plastic covers apart to eat the squishy plastic cupcakes inside.

Another hour went by, and we spent it snacking, checking the window, and getting to know each other a little better. Except for the fact that I was locked in a small cabin with one man and a few guns, with the possibility of scary monsters being right outside, it was a pleasant enough way to spend an evening. I'd had worse times with a guy, it was true.

Suddenly, we heard a commotion outside. It sounded like splashing followed by gravel being run through a garbage disposal. What the heck! We looked at each other, and then got up from our chairs to sneak over to the window. He pulled the curtain back ever so slightly, and we peered through it together. We were standing so close to each other that our shirtsleeves were touching. For a split second I imagined a spark igniting between us. I imagined our shirts falling in love and running off to Martinique together. Then I refocused and looked out the window. It was so dark, however, that I couldn't really see anything.

"Just there, do you see?" he whispered excitedly.

"I think so!" I said, not knowing what the heck I was

supposed to be looking at. I was terrified and excited, and also suddenly feeling very attracted to Danny. It had been there all along, I knew this, but only under the influence of alcohol, cupcakes, and the threat of death could I really admit it to myself. I tried to refocus and looked even harder out the window. "Oh!" I scream whispered. He smelled so damn good. Danny, not Bigfoot.

I saw something creeping along the tree line. It appeared to be a big, black, and possibly furry blob. The blob stopped to pick something up off the ground, held it up to its face, then looked left and right like it was about to cross a street. And then it disappeared back into the trees. I started breathing again. We both stood there for a few seconds, not saying anything, not moving. I was elated, confused, and scared out of my mind. I turned to Danny, and before I knew what was happening, he was kissing me.

His lips were soft, and they knew what they were doing and where they were supposed to go. I considered pulling back, but my girlie parts threatened my brain with an all-out revolt, and my brain acquiesced. We stayed that way for an hour, and I heard angels singing to harp music, and the clouds parted and rays of sunshine streamed through the room. At least it seemed like an hour. And I really do think I heard harp music coming from somewhere. But in reality, our kiss was brief. He pulled away from me slowly, kissing me once on the side of my neck before leaning back to look at me. His eyes were soft, and his lips were still parted. Oh, sweet baby Jesus, my knees were about to buckle.

"What in the great heavens above was that?" I asked as Danny let the curtain drop back in front of the window.

"I think they call that a kiss," he answered softly.

"No, I mean, yes. I mean, wait. No, the thing outside," I

tried to clarify, but the speech part of my brain was not yet working properly.

"Oh, that. Well, I'll give you three guesses," he said. "Come here." He took my hand, and we walked over to the chairs. He motioned for me to sit down, and I did, which was a good thing because it still felt like my legs were going to collapse. He picked up the laptop and sat on the arm of my chair, placing the computer in my lap. "Let's give this a look-see."

He leaned in to rewind and play the video, and I could hear him breathing, and suddenly my heartbeat became very loud in my ears and I thought maybe I would pass out. Was Danny more scary than seeing Bigfoot? Was that really even Bigfoot? Was he still out there? Why was Danny scary? His lips certainly weren't scary.

"Here we go," he mumbled, pointing to a spot on the screen. We watched the blob reach down to the ground and take off.

"I'm not really sure what I'm looking at," I commented as a true reporter would.

"I would think that it's obvious," he insisted.

"Not in the least! I couldn't tell if that was Bigfoot or Bob Hope," I exclaimed.

"Bob Hope is dead. And you can clearly see that Bigfoot wasn't wearing plaid golf pants."

"They *say* Bob Hope is dead, but they also say there is no such thing as Bigfoot."

"Well, we've got one on video, and you saw it for yourself, right out there," Danny huffed.

I tilted my head and rolled my eyes as a silent "meh" gesture. I was still taking the middle road—slightly terrified but skeptical as hell. I did see something, but it could have been anything. It could have been the same giant meatloaf that Al and Bill had seen. I wasn't going to admit anything either way. I had my doubts.

"Maybe we need to get one of those Bigfoot experts down in Honobia to verify this for us," I suggested, pointing to the laptop.

"Oh damn, Bev, those wahoos down there wouldn't know a Sasquatch from a hole in the ground. I'm telling you, we just saw Bigfoot!" He closed his laptop and folded his arms in front of his chest, satisfied that our work was now done.

"Okay, if you say so," I yawned. I already knew those Honobia experts were wahoos—everyone was. I suddenly felt very sleepy. It was close to two in the morning, and I was beat, and agreeing with Danny seemed like it would be the fastest way to get me home and into my own bed. I thought about that kiss. In bed. Nope! Don't go there! I shook my head to snap myself out of it. I needed to get home to bed—by myself. I didn't want to get carried away. I didn't want to make the same mistakes I had kept making in New York. I wanted to be smart this time, and I knew that things had to be handled differently in a small town. It was just a kiss, after all.

Danny watched me yawn. "Let's get you home and into bed," he said. "I mean, you know, your bed. Your home, with like, I mean, yeah." He was turning red.

"I know what you mean," I laughed. "Yes, let's pack up. I've definitely seen enough."

TWENTY

We began packing up our bags, and Danny blew out the candles and tidied up the kitchen. As we went to the door to leave, he pulled a rifle off the wall, checking the safety before placing it under his arm.

"What do we need that for?" I asked.

"We just saw a Bigfoot out there; he could still be around," he answered casually as he opened the door and ushered me outside.

I stopped in my tracks. "What the what?" I hadn't thought of this. Did I really want to walk back to the truck after just seeing a Bigfoot out there?

"Look, don't worry about it," Danny assured me. "The thing just had a snack, he's happy, probably took half back to his wife, I mean domestic partner. He's long gone by now. At least, I'm reasonably sure."

I eyed the rifle under his arm. "I'm just taking this with us to make you feel better," he confided.

I didn't believe him. "Right," I drawled.

He locked up the cabin, and we began walking back to

his truck. The moon was lower on the horizon and soon would be completely obscured by trees.

As we walked, I mentally replayed the surprise kiss. I definitely hadn't seen that coming, although I certainly didn't mind that it had. But what did it mean? Did I care? Kind of. Of course I would go straight to "what does it mean?" rather than simply enjoy what it was. Was it a trait of the female gender to wonder what something means, while the males simply moved on to the next piece of business—whatever that was? I knew what the answer was when it came to romance novels, but not when it came to real life. Maybe it was because I was a writer and had analyzed stories for a living. It was hard not to do that in real life, too.

I watched Danny leading the way in front of me. He had a light jacket on, his backpack over his shoulder and a gun under one arm. I watched the sway of his hips as he walked and listened to the sound of his boots on the path. Aw, to heck with where it was headed. It was a great kiss. I wouldn't mind more.

My stomach growled, and it pulled me out of my reverie. I guess I hadn't eaten anything with much substance over the course of the evening. I stuck a hand into the outside pocket of my backpack and pulled out a package containing two Hostess Cupcakes that Danny must have stuck in there before we left. Well, it was easier than searching through the whole bag for something healthier.

"So how do you feel, after having seen your first Bigfoot?" Danny asked, turning his head to the side so I could hear him.

"I feel suspicious," I said with a mouthful of cupcake.

He stopped in his tracks. "What do you mean?"

I waited till I had finished my mouthful of dessert to continue. "It was all too easy," I observed. "I mean, we just had to throw out a cupcake, wait a few hours, and presto! Fake monster." I was still a little shaken, but I was more skeptical than scared, and I wanted to prove it.

"I—that's ridiculous! You saw it with your own eyes. That wasn't fake!"

"I saw a dark blob across a dark clearing. And I saw a grainy dark blob in some grainy dark video footage. Proves nothing."

He looked slightly dejected, and I felt bad. "Look," I continued, "I am very grateful that you took time to bring me out here—really, I am! You're definitely very knowledgeable about Bigfoot, and I definitely have more material for my article. And I had a really nice time..." I thought about that kiss again. "But I'm not ready to admit I just saw a Bigfoot. Sorry." I shrugged and continued walking up the path.

I heard Danny's footsteps stop behind me, and I turned to face him. He had a strange look on his face.

"What?" I asked.

He sighed. "Okay, I can't lie to you. I thought it would be fun, but I guess I can't go through with it. You're right. That wasn't a Bigfoot."

Aha! I knew it! Vindication! Take that, Guthrie! I was happy and feeling so smug I wasn't even mad at him. I laughed.

"You're not mad?"

"Kind of," I bluffed. "But I just knew it! There's no way."

"Hey, now, don't get me wrong. Bigfoot most definitely does exist around here, and I have seen one. But of course, I wasn't sure we'd see one tonight, so I kind of made sure we did." He tossed his head, shaking a lock of hair out of his face. As if on cue, as if he knew I definitely couldn't be mad at someone who was working the cute so hard. It totally worked.

"All right." I said, my voice softening. "It was a fun night, for sure. And it's true, now I can go home saying I saw Bigfoot tonight." I took another bite of cupcake.

Danny laughed, and we continued our trek back to the truck. "You could pretend it was real and just write the article as if it was. That'll score you a lot of points, I'll bet. Both with the readers and your boss," he concluded.

"Already thought of that," I said happily. "The rest of the article is gonna be a snap!"

I got back to the truck before Danny did, and I leaned against the back tire on the passenger side to knock some dirt off my shoes when I heard a rustle in the trees just beyond the front of the truck. Just another raccoon, I decided, and continued to clean off my shoes. But then the rustling noise got louder, and then I distinctly heard the sound of a chicken clucking. I looked up just in time to see a dark figure walking toward me. It was very large and was holding something under one arm. It appeared to be hairy. And it was breathing very loudly. Danny's hired monster was still on the clock, apparently. Maybe that was his human clothes tucked under his arm. But I still couldn't account for the chicken clucks.

"Yeah, right, Danny. Once was enough; no need to overdo it," I complained loudly, and stood with one hip thrust out in defiance. The thing kept coming toward me. "It's all good, I already know you're fake. Aren't you tired? We can call it a night now," I told the guy in the hairy suit. Still it kept coming at me. It was close enough now that I could see its face. The beady black eyes were staring at my hands. Wow, I thought. That is a pretty convincing monster mask!

It was close enough that I could now see what was tucked under its arm. It was a chicken. It wasn't just any chicken though. It was Beryl. My jaw dropped. The guy kept looking at my hands, and I looked down to realize I was still holding one Hostess Cupcake.

"Oh, I get it," I said with plenty of smarm. "You're hungry! Well, I can't say as I blame you, having been out here all night." I took a step closer to him. "I tell you what. I'll make a deal with you."

I continued to walk up to him and held out my cupcake. "I'll trade you for the chicken."

The guy grabbed the cupcake from my hand and shoved my chicken at me. He stuffed the cupcake in his mouth and turned and ran back into the trees. Well, that was fun. Beryl was squirming under my arm, as usual. Welcome home, jailbird.

"Nice touch, Danny," I mocked as I turned around to face him. His face was white as a sheet. He stared at the chicken.

"Uh," he mumbled.

"What, don't have anything to say this time? You could have just called your guy to tell him he could go home early. But the chicken is a nice touch. What, did you steal her from my backyard earlier in the week as part of the plan for tonight?" I knew this wasn't true because Beryl had gone missing before I had arranged for the stakeout. But whatever. Now I was so mad it didn't really matter right this moment.

"Uh," Danny stammered again, not moving.

"Whatever," I mumbled, unimpressed. I was tired. "Where can I put this?" I asked grumpily, holding Beryl out in front of me like she was someone else's dirty socks.

Without saying a word, Danny took Beryl from me and put her in a crate that was in the bed of his truck. It was probably meant for dogs but was now holding a recaptured chicken.

I turned to get in the truck. "How do I get into this thing?" I wasn't in the mood to climb Mount Everest again, but I also wasn't in the mood to wait for Danny to open the door and help push me up and in. I took one last breath of lower-altitude oxygen and hoisted myself up.

He climbed in the truck, started the engine, and locked the doors. After we were down the road about a quarter of a mile, he finally spoke.

"So guess what," he said slowly. I looked at him, and his face was still devoid of color.

"What, are we meeting Bigfoot at your pool for a midnight swim and a nightcap?" I quipped.

"No, not exactly," he sighed. "That thing back there? That wasn't my friend."

I laughed again. "What are you saying exactly?"

"At the cabin. That was my friend Tom; he works on the ranch. That back *there*"—he pointed with his thumb to the road behind us—"was an actual Bigfoot."

"Yeah, right. That thing was as much a Sasquatch as my aunt Margaret is. And she's pretty hairy, but she ain't no Bigfoot. Did you see that costume? It was totally fake! I saw a zipper." I really wanted to remember seeing a zipper.

"You may want to do a DNA test on your aunt, then, because I'm one hundred percent serious—that was not Tom; that was a real effing Bigfoot."

Danny sure did sound insistent. Huh. I looked at him; his face was long, and his expression was serious. Oh.

"You mean..." I drawled.

"Yes."

"...I just gave my cupcake up to a real Sasquatch?"

"This is what I'm saying."

"And Bigfoot just gave me my chicken back?"

"You recognize this chicken?" Danny asked incredulously, jerking his head toward the back of the truck.

"Oh yes," I explained. "Beryl went missing on Thursday from a locked chicken coop in my backyard. And now you're telling me Bigfoot has just given her back?" My brain wasn't quite catching on yet. I couldn't think of anything else to say. Beryl was so much trouble that not even Bigfoot wanted her.

"It would appear so." Danny said. He looked like he was trying to mentally calculate the square root of 4,379,563,402.

"Huh. Well, at least he was polite." I had to give him that much.

"That's all you have to say?" It was as if he was expecting me to be freaked-out by having come in contact with a real live Bigfoot. Was I supposed to be shrieking at the top of my lungs? Or should I pass out? I was having a hard time believing I was this calm, too. I still wasn't entirely convinced it was real. But I just couldn't explain the chicken.

"No, I guess not," I said thoughtfully.

I turned toward him, searching his face for clues. His profile was lit by the instrument cluster in the dash, and I couldn't help staring at his lips. "First off, I don't believe that was really Bigfoot. Even you agreed it was too much of a coincidence to have seen one tonight. I still can't explain the chicken, though. But if that really was a Bigfoot, why on earth didn't you do something? You had a gun for cripes' sake. Were you just going to let him run off with me?" It was all becoming a little too much for my brain to handle, and I began to hyperventilate. Deep belly breaths. Long exhales. "I mean, he could have thrown me over his shoulder and run off with me!" I thought of all the things I hadn't done with my life yet. The novel writing. Finding the love of my life. Figuring out how to make a decent homemade pizza crust.

By this time we had driven up to Danny's house, and he turned to park in front of it. He cut the engine.

"Look," he said, turning toward me so we were face-to-face. He slid over to the middle of the seat so we were closer to each other. Now I was hyperventilating because of that.

"First off, I'm telling you, it was an actual, bona fide, real live Bigfoot. It was not a man in a suit. It does seem too good to be true, but—"

"Good is a relative term!" I exploded. "Good! That was not good!"

"Sure it was! You really did get everything you need for your article now—you have proof. Firsthand experience! And secondly, I was right behind you with the rifle. I couldn't get a good shot at him because you were blocking my line of fire. If he had tried anything, I would have rescued you. But see, it turned out okay. I told you they like cupcakes. They're just hungry. And curious. He probably thought you were cute." He sparkled those blue eyes at me and leaned closer. He looked away for a moment. "Although I sure can't explain the chicken, either," he added.

Oh. My. God. A real Bigfoot. Nope. No way. My breath became louder as I worked really hard to convince myself that it had been fake and Danny just wasn't coming clean about this setup. And there were those lips again. What a great distraction. He was so close that I could have just leaned over and kissed him. So I did. And I made this one count. Let's just say I forgot about Bigfoot, at least for a little while.

He reached out a hand and gently placed it on the back of my head. He ran his fingers through my curls, and I started to think we were having a contest to see who could go the longest without stopping for air. I knew if we stayed like this too long the mood would change to something a little more serious, and I was not ready to have that happen in the cab of a big giant monster truck. I was too old for that game.

I slowly, finally, pulled away.

"What was that for?" he mumbled.

"It was a test," I mumbled back.

"Did I pass?"

"I think so." I leaned back against the passenger door to get a good look at him and took in a deep breath. "Yup. Yes. You passed," I exhaled.

"Good." He smiled, slid back behind the wheel, and started his truck back up. "Let's get you and your chicken home," he said softly.

We were quiet for a while, and I was back to trying to wrap my head around what had happened. As we pulled out onto the main highway, he broke the silence.

"What test did I pass, exactly?"

I sighed. "I was wondering why you had kissed me back at the cabin. I thought maybe you had done it to try to distract me from the fact that Bigfoot was just your friend in a bear suit. I thought maybe a second try might help me get a little more clarity on the subject."

"I see," he said thoughtfully. "And you're sure I passed?"

"Not one hundred percent," I admitted. "I still don't believe it was real, so maybe all of this—" I waved my hand at the inside of the truck, not really sure what I was referring to. "—is just a distraction."

"Beverley," he began.

"Nope, don't want to hear it. But you're right about one thing: at least I've got some more material for my article." I was satisfied.

Out of the corner of my eye, I saw him shrug his shoulders. I shrugged mine, too.

"I do have one question for you, though," I added. It was time to lay it all out on the table.

"Shoot!" he said eagerly.

"Were you by any chance on I-35 south of town this afternoon?" I squeezed my eyes shut, waiting for his answer. I didn't really want to know, but I really wanted to know.

"Hmm," he pondered. "Let me think now."

The suspense was driving me crazy.

"Hmm," he said again.

"It should be pretty easy to remember, I'd think. Unless you suffer from short-term memory loss?"

He laughed. "No, I wasn't on I-35 at all today. Had stuff to do on the ranch. How come?"

"Oh, no reason," I said slowly, relief seeping into my voice and combining with exhaustion. I saw him silently shake his head out of the corner of my eye.

Twenty minutes later he had dropped me off at my house, after I heartily insisted I really could walk over to the *Ledger* building on Sunday to retrieve my car. I thanked him again for the entertainment, and he handed over my chicken and gave me an almost chaste peck on the cheek. It was not fully chaste, just slightly, because I picked up a definite sultry undertone as his lips brushed against my cheek. At least I think I did, and anyway, it felt good to imagine some nonchaste thoughts in there somewhere.

I locked up Beryl with her friends, who didn't seem all that happy to see her home. I shut the pen as tightly as I could, knowing that if Bigfoot got in once to steal my Beryl, then he could probably do it again and there wasn't much I could do to stop him.

I then headed into the house and locked everything up. As I got ready for bed, I reflected on the excitement of the evening. The kiss, the guy in a hairy suit, the return of the prodigal hen, and the fact that I hadn't gotten to finish my cupcakes. I went to bed with my stomach growling.

TWENTY-ONE

SUNDAY MORNING FOUND me up early, having risen with my automatic alarm clocks, aka the chickens. I went out to check the coop—it was still locked up, and everyone was accounted for. Beryl seemed quieter than she usually was. Maybe she was humbled by her time as a Bigfoot captive. Perhaps she realized she was damn lucky not to have been eaten. Maybe she was even happy to be home. It was a stretch but still possible.

I went for a short run—to retrieve my car. I had a shower and a small breakfast, and after consuming an obscenely large amount of coffee, I got to work on the Bigfoot article, which was due by six. It went surprisingly fast. I wasn't sure if it was because I had put more of a rough draft together than I thought, or if suddenly everything came together once I had spent a night out in the wilderness and gotten scared out of my wits by what may or may not have been a real live specimen. In either case I was done by noon. The words just flowed, and I wrote them down as they came. It was as if I was finally channeling my inner Guthrie resident. I started to believe that everything might just work out after all. Even the title practically wrote itself: AREA BIGFOOT SIGHT-INGS LEAVE BIG IMPRESSION ON LOCALS.

After reading it through several times, I shut my eyes and hit Send on the email to Mark. I felt a huge wave of relief wash over me. I was done. I knew I might have more unusual assignments like this in the future, but I was glad I had this one over with. And I hoped that now I would be able to steer clear of Bigfoot—at least for a while. I checked the time on my phone. I had just enough time to eat a little lunch, bake a cheesecake, and take a nap before Kelly's barbecue.

Around 2:00 p.m., my phone buzzed. It was a text from Mark. My stomach tightened—he usually only texted with something bad, like giving me a thirty-minute window to write a last-minute story about embezzlement in the quilting guild, or something equally as scandalous. With trepidation, I peeked at the text.

Mark: *good job*.

I gasped. This was high praise, coming from him! I thought about texting him back with "Are you sure? Because I was kind of scared that you wouldn't like it and then fire me, but please don't because I really want this job and I tried as hard as I could." But then I thought better of it and decided not to write back at all. Yeah. The less said the better. I'd see him in a few hours at Kelly's, anyway.

Maybe I was finally making some headway, I thought, as I pulled a perfect, golden-brown cheesecake out of the oven. Maybe I could get the hang of this small-town journalism thing, and maybe I could really be part of the community. Maybe it was all easier than I had made it out to be. I felt hopeful.

With the scent of freshly baked dessert wafting through

the house, I collapsed on the couch and immediately fell asleep. I did have the presence of mind to set an alarm on my phone before I crashed, so it was kind of a miracle that I managed to be awake, showered, and dressed by the time my doorbell rang at 5:15.

"Hiya," Danny said as I opened the door. "Wow." He continued as he looked me over. "You look great."

I looked down at my white T-shirt, jeans with the cuffs rolled up, and my sockless feet nestled in my favorite pair of Vans. Hmm. Maybe my nap refreshed me to the point of looking fabulous! Well, it was a long shot, but it was possible. Maybe he just liked Vans. I felt myself blushing, and suddenly I was tongue-tied. "Me too," I blurted out. "I mean, you do. Wait." Maybe I was still more tired than I thought.

He laughed and stepped into the house. "Are you ready to go?"

"I just need to get the cake," I said over my shoulder as I walked to the kitchen to get the dessert. When I came back into the living room, he was still standing by the door, looking at my wall of bookshelves. "Ready," I said as I walked up beside him. I handed him the plate and ushered him back through the door as I picked up the bag containing some beer.

"So how did the article turn out?" he asked expectantly.

"Well," I answered coyly as I could, "you'll just have to wait until next week's paper comes out, like everyone else."

"Damnit, I figured you'd say something like that."

"Don't drop that cake," I warned.

We drove to Kelly's in his giant monster truck and spent the evening in her backyard with our friends. The food was delicious, the weather was flawless, and everyone was in a good mood—even Mark. The sun went down, and we continued to lounge outside, enjoying the ideal late-summer evening. In a matter of weeks, the breeze would turn cold and the leaves would begin to change, signaling the coming of winter. But for now, for this one warm, perfect evening, we all silently acknowledged this fleeting moment of perfection. My shoulders relaxed, and I could feel a sense of relief washing over me. It was as if the stress from the past week finally just left my body all at once. It was over.

I was still terrified of Bigfoot, and I probably always would be. But I had faced my fear, and all that happened was I lost a cupcake—but I did regain a chicken. I had survived, and for that I was incredibly happy.

I had spent the last week on edge while faced with a deadline from my cranky boss. I had had to interview my landlady and her crazy friends. I had, however, met a really nice guy—a definite bright spot. I watched Danny as he talked with Ben about some kind of sportsing event. He took a swig of his beer and looked over at me. We shared a moment. Yes, he had been a definite highlight in a truly weird, stressful week. I sighed contentedly.

Maybe I was finally settling in, or maybe life just seemed that much sweeter after surviving a face-to-face encounter with a cupcake-eating beast. Had it really been Bigfoot? Would I ever know? Unsure. But this evening, it didn't seem to matter much one way or the other. I looked up and saw stars between the tree branches, and my breath caught slightly. Suddenly I had an answer to that question I'd been asking for the last few months. Suddenly I was totally and completely sure why I had moved back to Oklahoma and made my home in Guthrie. As I sat with my friends, laughter sweeping across the yard on the warm breeze, the answer was clear. I was truly home.

Want some cool Beverley Green merchandise? Visit "Beverley Green's Guthrie Mercantile" on Society6 for the latest and greatest!

Visit today: www.society6.com/acneil

ACKNOWLEDGMENTS

Thanks to my parental units, always my biggest fans—my mom from way up high, my dad from his kitchen table.

Thanks to Marcus, for all the cappuccinos and for keeping my feet on the ground.

Vielen Dank to my Wise Aunt Deepti, for all the encouragement and project management skillz.

Huge thanks to Punk Rock Breann, Wordy Girl Ren, Zazzy Cynthia, and SuperDayl – the best dang girlfriends a weirdo could have.

Thanks to those who took the time to help me with valuable feedback – Danielle, Michele, Connie, Mary, and Roberta.

Much metta to my yoga family, who has had to listen to me go on and on about writing a book (and guess what guys, there's more to come!)

And to all the Unicorns out there – yeah, you – keep on spreading those rainbows.

ABOUT THE AUTHOR

Andrea has been writing stories since forever but has only recently managed to write a coherent long one, and is just now getting around to publishing it. Often reaching for the lighter side of heavier stuff, her stories include a hefty dose of sass, a smidge of whimsy and a whole lot of quirkiness. Andrea also blogs on various topics including how to be a professional introvert, ways to cultivate your dry wit, and how to cleanse your chakras by drinking the right kind of smoothie.

Born and raised in Southern California, Andrea frequently did her homework on the beach while watching waves and surfers. She currently lives in Tulsa, Oklahoma with her partner and a whole bunch of air plants. When not writing, Andrea teaches yoga and enjoys knitting, drinking coffee, and cursing at television commercials.

 facebook.com/andreacneil

twitter.com/acaitneil

 instagram.com/acaitneil

Made in the USA
Lexington, KY
23 September 2018